10-99

	DATE DUE		

Winner of the Carolina Novel Award

The Carolina Novel Award was established in 1996 by Banks Channel Books to recognize excellence in fiction writing by Carolina authors. It is awarded to the author of a previously unpublished manuscript chosen in open competition.

Styles By

Maggie Sweet

by

Judith Minthorn Stacy

To Ben
Roger
Linda
Michael
Christopher
and their families,
with love

Acknowledgments

I would like to thank the following, whose encouragement has been invaluable to me. My father, Robert Minthorn, the first to suggest I try writing and one of the few who still calls me "kid," and my stepmother, Mary.

I thank my sisters, Joanne Clark, Margaret Yu, Nancy Toler and Susan Gornichec, for their unfailing support and forever friendship.

My ninety-nine-year-old grandmother, Alma Ellen MacDonald, whose endurance and humor continue to delight and surprise me.

In ways I don't understand, this story is connected to the memory of my mother, Ethel Minthorn; my sister, Linda Minthorn Kehl; my son, Mark Stacy; my grandson, Scott Miller; and my mother-in-law, Georgia B. Stacy.
I am indebted to my teachers, Lila McGinness, and the late Virginia Christenbury, who inspired me to keep writing.

I would like to thank my writer's group, Thursday's Child, who helped me find, tell, and publish this story.
Special thanks to Phyllis Supnick, Glenys Bailey, Peggy Patterson, and Gypsy Travis, for their faithful and long-standing friendship.

Finally, I am deeply grateful to Ellyn Bache, whose patient editing and enthusiastic response to my work made publishing this book a reality.

Chapter 1

April 2, 1985

ATTENTION: AUNT SALLY CARES
THE DAILY RIPPLE
Barium Springs, North Carolina

Dear Aunt Sally,

This is the first time I ever wrote to anyone for advice, but I have studied and studied, and I swear I don't know what else to do. Last night at supper my husband announced that he had taken our entire life savings and spent it on a family cemetery plot.

Aunt Sally, I'm only 38 years old. Why, just that morning I'd been thinking that when my girls graduate from high school this June maybe I could start to live a little.

We had even talked about using that money for something fun, like a family vacation to Myrtle Beach. Just daydreaming about what we'd do with all that money really kept me going some days.

I never, in all my life, thought he was thinking about cemetery plots!

Well, to make a long story short, when he told me what he'd done, I got all torn up, right there at the kitchen table, in front of everyone.

The way I see it, he had no right to spend all that money without talking it over with me.

He said I should be relieved to know that I'd be taken care of for all of eternity.

I cannot tell you how discouraging those words were to me.

Now don't get me wrong; my husband is a good man. But when he told me I'd be spending all of eternity resting beside him at All Souls Cemetery, right here in Poplar Grove, North Carolina, I got slicing pains in my chest.

I always thought something was going to happen sooner or later. Now I keep thinking, what if this is all there is slam up to and even after death? An everlasting eternity of nothing ever happening but the same old tired routine

If this is true, I'm desperate. Please tell me what to do before it's too late.

The Teachers Wife

Dear T. W.

It sounds to me like you think too much. You need to stay busy. Join the PTA, teach Sunday school, take up Bingo. Get creative. Enclosed is a copy of "The Joys Of Jello" cookbook guaranteed to open up a whole new world of cuisine to you and your family. Perfect tiered Jello rings, multicolored ribbon salads and scrumptious Jello strawberry pie. This will add so much excitement and variety to your life, you'll wonder how you got along without it. Especially when you see the looks of gratitude on your family's faces.

Remember you could do worse than to have a husband who knows where he's going in this world and the next. Believe me, I know.

Always remember Aunt Sally Cares.

Until recently I'd have called myself a typical small-town southern housewife. You know, bored, but resigned to the whole thing.

But things just kept going from bad to worse until I couldn't hardly take it anymore. That's when I decided to write to Aunt Sally Cares in the Barium Springs *Daily Ripple*, who used to give good advice, but lately sounds more and more like some throwback to the fifties.

(I mean *The Joys of Jello!* You've got to be kidding! But what choice did I have? If I wrote to the *Poplar Grove Expositor* sure as shooting someone would have recognized me. To tell you the truth, it's almost impossible to have any secrets in a small town.)

It's easier to write to a paper over in Barium Springs since not a living soul over there knows me. It's also just close enough that if I was to run into anyone from home, I'd just say I was there for the Red Star Superette's Grand Opening Two-For-One sale. It would never come to anyone that a person would drive that far for just a *Ripple*.

Well, after all that driving—it took three trips and about two tanks of gas before my letter appeared in the paper—Aunt Sally gave me the same advice my own Mama Dean would have given me right here at home, for free.

Still, it was weirdest thing. Aunt Sally's advice had no sooner appeared in the evening paper than my telephone started ringing right off the wall. All at once I'd gone from bored to being busier than a one armed paper-hanger.

First, my best friend Mary Price Bumbalough called to tell me that our high school was having its twentieth class reunion this summer. Mary Price's phone call shook me up but good, 'cause from what she said, all of our old classmates are leaving home, taking lovers and seemed to know how to live.

So there I was standing in my very own kitchen, talking on my very own phone with Mary Price going on and on about the reunion, when it suddenly came to me like a flash! There is more to life than collecting Tupperware and keeping the sourdough alive and every one of my old classmates already knew it. I was the only one who was sleepwalking through life.

I wondered if it was because I'd stayed behind in Poplar Grove, while the rest of them had seen the world. Why, they'd lived in cities like Raleigh, Winston-Salem, Charlotte—you name it!

Of course, Mary Price never got out of Poplar Grove either and she still lives an exciting life. But then that's Mary Price. Not only does she have a house, a husband, and two kids, she and Hoyt sing and play country music every weekend at the That'lldu Bar & Grill. She's also taken to parading all over town dressed in cowgirl outfits complete with hats and boots. When I told her people were starting to talk about her she just laughed. Mary Price is absolutely fearless.

The more I thought about Mary Price and Hoyt and everyone else who graduated with me, the more I wanted to add some excitement to my own life. But I swan, what with one thing and another, I just wasn't sure how to get started. I mean, just how far can a nice Methodist girl from Poplar

Grove, North Carolina, go? Especially, when you consider all the obstacles in my way.

First, there's my husband Steven. Steven is a high school biology teacher who makes love only when his vas tubes are blocked. The only time he "spent money like a drunken sailor" was when he bought the cemetery plots.

Next, there are my twin teenage daughters, Amy and Jill.

Amy is a clean, wholesome, honor-roll student. She wears a smooth shoulder-length bob, cultured pearls, and preppy clothes. Her goal in life is to get into an expensive college, marry someone worthy of her, and leave tacky us and tacky Poplar Grove far behind. Why, even Mama Dean, her great-grandmother, says Amy's got more airs than an electric fan.

And Jill. For three years, Jill dressed in an army shirt with the name PFC Presson emblazoned on the pocket. Then, last year, she saw an Indian on TV who sold chain-saw art out of the back of a truck in the parking lots of malls. Next thing we knew, Jill was wearing her blonde hair in a fat braid, dressing like Hiawatha and dedicating her life to dragging logs, branches, sometimes whole dead trees home to the garage workshop.

Also, there's my Mother and Mama Dean, who live three blocks away. Mother is a crisp, no-nonsense Licensed Practical Nurse, while Mama Dean is suspicious and high-tempered. They only have two things in common: a deep and abiding mistrust of men and keeping an eye on me.

So besides being Methodist, my family is a big part of why I never learned how to throw caution to the wind and really live.

Well, as if I wasn't already shook up enough, I'd just hung up with Mary Price when the telephone rang again.

It was another old classmate who had never left Poplar Grove either. Dreama Goforth. Actually Dreama Goforth Nims since she married poor old Bucky Nims. (Bucky owns Nims Hardware down on Main Street.)

Twenty years ago, Dreama Goforth was the biggest gossip in the entire Poplar Grove school system. Now she's the biggest gossip in all of Poplar Grove. And to make matters worse she pretends she's Miss Holy Christian.

Naturally, the minute I heard who it was, I put up my guard. The first thing out of Dreama's mouth was that she was in charge of the reunion ticket committee. This didn't surprise me one bit since this way she can find out everything about everyone who's coming.

After pussy-footing around for awhile, Dreama finally asked, "How many tickets are you gonna need for the reunion, Maggie Sweet? One ticket, just for yourself, or will Steven be coming along with you?"

Since I wasn't sure what she was getting at, I was real careful. "Why Dreama, you know I'll need two tickets. Steven and I do absolutely everything together." Which of course is a lie, but I'd rather hang out wash on a wet day than tell *her* any different.

"Well, I think that's just wonderful, Maggie Sweet," Dreama purred. "I'll just put you down for two tickets then."

For a minute, I relaxed and let down my guard and then she said, "Oh, by the way, hon, you'll never guess who I just talked to."

"I'm sure I couldn't say, Dreama." My voice just as cool and disinterested as can be.

"Well, the least you can do is guess," she said, and I could just picture her bottom lip pooching out in a pout.

When I still didn't say anything she sighed real loud

right into the receiver. "All right! All right! I'll tell you. But you better sit down."

"Dreama, please. I'm just real busy right now."

Then she hit me with it. "All right Maggie Sweet, but I warned you. I've only been talking to your old flame, Jerry Roberts, that's all!" She paused for a minute to let that sink in.

Well, I guess I should have sat down. For a minute I felt like someone had cut off my air.

"You'll just never guess what he told me," she went on. "Him and that wife of his are separated and he wouldn't miss this reunion for anything in the world! He is ab-so-lute-ly dying to see you, hon."

By now I was barely breathing at all. But Dreama just kept chattering away so I was pretty sure she didn't know how hard this had hit me.

"Maggie Sweet, it'll be just like old times. You and Jerry together after all these years. I wonder what he looks like. I wonder what he'll think of you. Maggie Sweet, are you there, hon? Now just what was it you were saying darlin'? Did you say you wanted old Steven to come along or did you just want one ticket for yourself after all?"

Dreama Goforth Nims is a nosy, interfering old busy-body, and I purely despise her, but she sure can ask some questions.

It was later, when I was breading meat for country fried steaks for supper, that I wondered how I'd answered her. I think I said I'd call her back. But I wasn't sure. Because even after all these years when I thought about Jerry Roberts I ran slam out of breath.

That night, I didn't get a wink of sleep. All night, I had this feeling that soon, very soon, my life was going to make a big change. But, to tell the Lord's truth, I'm not sure if I was more thrilled or scared about the whole thing. Finally, around five a.m. Steven rolled over in the bed and started snoring, so I gave up and tiptoed downstairs to start the coffee.

When the coffee was ready, I carried a mug out to the glider under the magnolia tree, my favorite thinking-things-over spot.

For awhile, I just sat there, drinking coffee and swinging and thinking about what had happened to all my old classmates and what had happened to me. But it all just kept going round and round in circles in my mind. So I decided to go clear back to the beginning.

I was baptized at the Pea Hill Methodist Church in Raleigh, North Carolina, thirty-eight years ago. Everyone says I look younger 'cause I'm small, have a Sally Field face, and hardly any bust.

Steven, my husband, was my high school biology teacher in 10th grade. But in those days I only thought of him as a teacher. The only reason he stuck out in my mind at all is because he blushed. I thought a grown man blushing was real sweet. But, he was the teacher. It would never have come to me to feel *that way* about a teacher.

No. The real love of my life all through school was Jerry Roberts. I thought Jerry had hung the moon.

But I'm getting way ahead of myself.

I'm the only child of Betty and Jack Sweet. When I was four, Mother brought complete disgrace on the family by divorcing Daddy after he took up drinking in Seoul, Korea, during the war. Mother said Daddy just wasn't the same and she was real sorry but she just couldn't live that way.

That's when Mother and I went to live at Mother's mother—my Mama Dean's—boarding house here in Poplar Grove.

One of my first memories, after we moved, was overhearing Mama Dean tell a neighbor that my daddy was really dead. Since she considered death much more fitting than divorce, she figured telling everyone he was dead was the best way to ward off gossip. At the age of four, I hadn't figured out how her mind worked, so I thought Daddy really was dead. Naturally, I had a pure fit and went screaming to Mother. And to Mama Dean's everlasting shame Mother carried me from house to house and told everyone the truth.

Smilin' Jack Sweet, as my daddy was called, stayed in touch. Once a month he'd drive from Raleigh to see me. We had dinners at truck-stops, then on to drive-in movies in his old Ford pick-up. Sometimes he'd even let me drive the truck. Since I was too little to reach the pedals, I'd sit on his lap and steer while he did the foot-work. 'Course he only let me drive in safe places like parking lots, but even so, I knew better than to tell Mother or Mama Dean.

We saw movies like *Mighty Joe Young* and *Francis the Talking Mule*. He'd let me drink RC cola right from the bottle while he drank something (which I now know was white lightning) from a bottle hidden in a brown paper sack in the glove-box. Daddy must have taken me to every carnival and fair in that part of the state. Sometimes he'd buy me so much cotton candy and Co'cola I'd be sick.

Since my everyday life with Mother was made up of Walt Disney movies, early bedtimes and foods from the four basic food groups, my visits with Daddy seemed downright reckless.

Daddy had nicknames for me. He called me "Rebel" or his "feisty little brown-haired girl." I loved it and begged him to call me "Scout" after being told that I looked like the little girl in *To Kill A Mockingbird*. Scout never caught on, but his other nicknames made me feel that Daddy saw something bold and spirited in me, something no one else seemed to notice.

Then I grew up. One Saturday, when I was about thirteen, Daddy appeared early, smelling of Wrigley's spearmint, Chesterfields, and Aqua Velva. He looked downright boyish the way he was grinning from ear to ear. He told me the circus was in town and he had taken the whole day off so we could go.

'Course now that I was a teenager, I thought I was much too old for childish things like the circus. I wanted to do what I considered mature things, like shopping for makeup and jewelry at Woolworths, and seeing the new Elvis movie uptown.

I was just about to tell him this when I saw the pride in his face. A look that said he'd saved a long time to give me this special outing. After that, I always acted excited over anything he wanted to do.

So, even though I knew Daddy drank too much, changed jobs too often, and would probably never grow up, I also knew he loved me just about better than anyone. Because when it was time to drop me off at the boarding house he'd say, "See ya' around fart-blossom," his voice all gruff and casual-like. But now, I saw the tears in his eyes when he said it.

Between Mother's pay as an LPN at Providence Hospital and Mama Dean's two little old-maid teacher boarders, we got by. They agreed to let Smilin' Jack visit because, "After all, he is her Daddy." Later they'd question me about where he had taken me and how much he had spent, with a satisfied, "I might have known, the pig," attitude. So if the grown-ups in my life were completely opposite, it was never boring for too long.

And then Jerry Roberts came into my life.

We met at a sock-hop in the high school gym the summer before our junior year in high school. I was standing on the side-lines talking to Mary Price and some other girls, when I heard, "Do you want to dance?"

When I turned, our eyes locked and it was like we were the only two people in the gym. I don't even know if I answered him, I just remember stepping into his arms as if I'd always known him, as if I'd been waiting for him my whole life. I wanted to say, "Do you *know* me? I *know* you, I've *known* you forever."

He was purely fascinating to my half-reckless, half-rule-abiding sixteen-year-old mind. He was my age, but seemed older: drove a souped-up '48 Chevy too fast, wore a ducktail haircut, carried his Marlboros in the rolled-up sleeve of his T-shirts, and had no curfew. (I loved to think of him as an outlaw.) And as if that wasn't enough, he had the most beautiful face I'd ever seen, eyes as blue and velvety as pansies, and (wonder of wonders) *he liked me too.*

But what really got me, what I'll never forget, is that we could talk about everything for hours. And sometimes, Jerry my sweet outlaw, read poetry to me.

Of course, everyone else only saw Jerry's outlaw side. The first time he drove me home from school with the radio blaring and the glass-pack muffler roaring, Mama Dean, who was drinking iced tea and watching *Search for Tomorrow*, must have come out of her chair like it had given her an electric shock. She went right to the porch light switch and flicked it off and on, my signal to get in the house pronto. When I ignored this signal, which was impossible to see on a bright October afternoon, she threw the old couch afghan around her shoulders and marched out to the driveway.

"Maggie Sweet! What do you think you're doing?" she said, her jaw stuck out and her eyes blazing.

"We were just talking, Mama Dean," I stammered.

"Hmph," she said. "That's your tale and I'm a' settin' on mine."

After she hauled me red-faced and wailing into the house she went straight to the phone and called Mother at work. In a high, hysterical voice, she said, "Betty, get home. Some rampageous wolf in sheep's clothing is fixin' to carry off our baby."

And Mother came straight home and tried to talk some sense into my head.

Nothing like this had ever happened before. Mother never took time off work for anything. That's how torn up they were over me seeing Jerry.

Until then, I'd mostly done what they said, but I would have walked through fire to be with Jerry.

Between Mother's speeches of "Listen to me, I'm your Mother," and Mama Dean's glinty-eyed tales about my philandering grandfather who had deserted her years before, I met Jerry every chance I got.

For two years it went on this way. Mother was sure that sooner or later her sensible genes would surface and I wouldn't go back on my raising. But Mama Dean, ever mindful of my grandfather's taint, followed me everywhere. Since we never owned a car, she was hard to miss. Sometimes during school I'd get that prickly feeling you get when someone is watching you. I'd glance out the window just in time to see a short, stocky woman in a flowered house-dress, disappear into the Red-Tip bushes.

Once, coming out of a movie (*Psycho*, I think) Jerry swore he saw an old woman in pink fuzzy house-shoes dart between parked cars.

Finally, one day, I caught her. I was in Dixie Burger, having a Coke with some friends, when a gray head peeked through a window, not two inches from my face, then disappeared. I marched out of the shop and found Mama Dean crawling around on all fours pretending to dig in the dirt.

"Mama Dean!" I shrieked.

"Hey, Maggie Sweet," she said, grinning like she'd been caught with her hand in the collection plate. "I think I lost my house key."

This time I said, "Hmph!" and went straight home and bawled to Mother. "You've got to stop her. She's ruining my life."

Mother said, "Oh, foot, Maggie Sweet!" But she did talk to Mama Dean, who said, "All right! All right! But don't come to me when her tail gets full of burrs and expect me to curry them out."

So, Mama Dean quit following me and tried to be satisfied with reading my diary, listening in on my phone calls, and getting Miss Skurlock, my homeroom teacher and one of our boarders, to spy on me.

And after two years of just kissing and petting (above the waist but not under the clothes) my outlaw-poet was making his own demands.

"Do you love me?" he'd ask, trying to get his hand under my angora sweater.

"You know I do," I'd say truthfully, slapping his hand away.

"Then prove it," he'd say. "I'm only human. I'll still

respect you." As his hands went everywhere and wrestled me to the car floor.

I'd end up crying, and Jerry would say he was sorry. But the very next date was another pure wrestling match.

It finally got so bad that during our senior year we broke up almost every weekend. All this had my nerves so torn to pieces I cried all the time.

Then, on Monday, after breaking up Saturday night, there he'd be, waiting for me at my locker, like always. Even though he never said it, I could tell he was sorry. Why, three separate times that spring he gave me a rose and a Baby Ruth. Just like that old song from the fifties, "A Rose and a Baby Ruth." Now if that's not sorry, I don't know what is.

Our last date, the week before graduation, was prom night. Because of my curfew we'd left the prom early so we'd have time to make out at Belews Pond. But this time, when one thing led to another, Jerry wouldn't stop, even though I cried several times. It got so bad, I just couldn't control myself. The only thing I could do was to get out of the car and start walking up that dark country road, in my turquoise prom gown and strappy high heels, turning my ankles on every rock, and crying my eyes out.

The next thing I knew, Jerry was following me in the car, driving real slow, staying even with me. But I was too broken up to so much as look at him. Then, I heard his voice. It was so low and hoarse I could hardly tell it was him.

"Get back in the car, Maggie Sweet. For the Lord's sake, please get back in the car."

I will never, in all my life, forget how he sounded that night.

When we got back to my house, I told him we

couldn't go on that way and gave him back his class ring.

I cried all week, even in school. I waited, hoping he'd come to my locker like always. But this time he didn't. I lost five pounds and was jumpy as a cricket. Kind of like Natalie Wood in *Splendor In The Grass* when Warren Beatty wouldn't take "no."

All I could think of was getting Jerry back, so I made up my mind. If I wanted him back I had to do something daring. Even if it meant hardening my heart to Mama Dean's tragic broken figure, and the hurt in Mother's eyes, graduation night, I'd do it. I'd give myself to Jerry.

Chapter Two

Graduation day dawned hot and bright. I woke early, too excited to sleep. But even after I was awake, I stayed in my room a long time trying to memorize every detail of this important day. I heard the whir of the electric fan, Mother and Mama Dean's voices coming up through the kitchen air-vent. The curtains stirred at the opened window and the sun cast shadows on the blue forget-me-not wallpaper. I breathed in the crisp new smell of the yellow polished-cotton graduation dress Mother and I had bought on a shopping trip to Lerner's in Charlotte. My face in the mirror was pink with excitement, and I told myself to remember the light, the sounds, the heat, the very air of this June morning. Because, tonight, when I came back to this room, nothing would be the same.

After I dressed, I dabbed Tangee Natural on my lips and Vaseline on my eyelashes. Then I thought about the Maybelline cake mascara and Fire-Cracker red lipstick Mary Price and I had bought at Woolworths and hid in the back of my chifforobe. It would be the perfect day to try them.

Then I remembered our principal, Mr. Fentress', announcement over the PA during graduation practice: "No earrings, teased-up hair or loud makeup for graduation. Y'all are suppose to look like fresh young ladies, not New York City si-reens." We all laughed at the way he had said sirens, but there was no doubt in our minds he'd send us home to change, even on graduation day.

So I used extra Tangee and hoped for the best. At the last minute I sneaked into Mother's room and dabbed some Evening In Paris behind my ears. If I couldn't look like a si-reen, at least I could smell like one.

Mother and Mama Dean were putting pink rosettes on my red velvet cake when I finally came downstairs in my cap and gown. They'd even decorated the living room with red and gray crepe paper streamers, Poplar Grove's school colors.

"You'll be getting your biggest surprise later," Mama Dean said, winking at Mother.

I was too busy thinking about my surprise for Jerry to ask any questions.

When our class marched up the aisle to "Pomp and Circumstance," I could see Mother and Mama Dean seated near the front of the auditorium, fanning themselves with, IN YOUR TIME OF NEED CALL SIM'S FUNERAL HOME, cardboard fans.

Mama Dean bawled so loud everyone turned and stared at her as I walked across the stage for my diploma. Mother, who looked cool even in 90 degree heat, sat straight in her chair and looked prouder than I'd ever seen her.

For a minute, I felt guilty as homemade sin for what I was planning to do later. But the minute Jerry's blue eyes met mine across that crowded stage, I knew tonight had to be *the* night.

When we got back to the house for the family party, Smilin' Jack's new pick-up was parked in the driveway. Daddy was married to a nice country woman named Willa Mae now. They both had steady jobs at a hosiery mill and had bought a cute little house on the outskirts of Chapel Hill.

Daddy was getting downright respectable.

For my graduation present, he and Willa Mae gave me a complete Blue Waltz perfume set, dusting powder and all. Mother and Mama Dean had gone in together and got me a Bulova watch. Miss Honeycutt and Miss Skurlock, our boarders, gave me a mustard seed necklace (If you have the faith of a grain of mustard seed...*Matthew 17*) and a Cross pen and pencil set.

Then, over cake and punch, Smilin' Jack told me about my graduation surprise.

He'd paid my tuition, in full, to Chapel Hill School of Licensed Practical Nursing. He'd even found me a summer job at a Tastee-Freeze near his house. I'd be moving in with him and Willa Mae within the hour!

I grinned nervously at Mother and Mama Dean, sure that any minute one of them would say that Daddy was just teasing or that this was just another one of his "damn-fool notions." But the smile quickly died on my lips. Mother and Mama Dean were actually packing my suitcases.

"Maggie Sweet, we've been so worried about your future," they both said, their voices high with emotion, their eyes bright with tears.

I was really leaving. My future had been decided.

Even now, I can hardly believe that I did exactly what I was told. But that's how it was back then. Except for sneaking around to see Jerry and smoking Kools with Mary Price, I did what I was told. It just never came to me to do any different.

Besides, I don't think I really believed it was happening. For years, I'd had my whole life planned out. And

Lord knows, being a nurse and leaving Poplar Grove were not in my plans at all. Everyone knew that all I wanted in the world was to marry Jerry and go to The College of Cosmetology on Bud Hollings Street behind the Western Auto.

I even planned to have my own shop in the back of our house some day. I'd call it "Styles By Maggie Roberts". Now, you've got to admit that has a nice ring to it.

I spent entire study halls writing 'Mrs. Jerry Roberts' and 'Styles By Maggie Roberts' over and over in the margins of all my spiral notebooks.

Why, I'd been in love with Jerry for years and doing hair since I had to stand on a chair to reach. By the time I was twelve I was trimming bangs, giving Tonis, the works. I was good at it, too. Everybody said I had a real flair. They even rhymed it. "Maggie Sweet has the flair—for fixin' your hair!" I thought that sounded good, like the commercial "Winston tastes good—like a cigarette should."

When I was sixteen, I got a part-time job as a shampoo girl at Shirley's Curl & Swirl, the busiest shop in town. I loved the scent of Sea Breeze and Apple-pectin shampoo, the clutter of brush rollers, double-prong curl clips, and Dippity-Do; the mingled hum of Bonat hair dryers, women's voices and laughter. I loved it when plain little women handed Shirley pictures of stars like Sophia Loren, Grace Kelly, Elizabeth Taylor, saying, "I want to look like that."

Shirley would wink at me and whisper, "Who don't?"

Then she'd tease and curl and spray, and somehow the customer grew hair and confidence right before my eyes.

I'm not sure what I loved the most—Shirley and the

other beauticians treating me like I was the same age as they were or watching customers float out of the shop, looking good and knowing it.

When Shirley told me I had the gift, I thought I'd died and gone to beauty heaven.

Now here I was about to become a nurse. About to trade brush-rollers for bedpans.

During all the confusion of packing, I tried to sneak a phone call to Jerry.

Nice girls didn't call boys in those days, and we weren't even going steady anymore, but I was desperate. I let the phone ring and ring, but nobody ever answered.

By the time I called Mary Price, I was crying so hard, I could hardly talk. I figured if anyone could get me out of this it was Mary Price. But the only thing she could think of was stealing her Daddy's truck and the two of us running away. When she started bawling too, I knew I was stuck. But Mary Price promised to call Jerry for me and to write every day.

All the way to Chapel Hill, Daddy tried to cheer me up by telling knock-knock jokes. But all I could do was stare out the truck window and cry. I kept hoping it was all a bad dream, that any minute I'd wake up.

Later when I'd settled in with Daddy and Willa Mae, I wondered how Mother and Mama Dean had guessed about my graduation surprise for Jerry. They had to have guessed. In all my 18 years they'd never sent me home with Daddy before.

Mary Price, who was going steady with Hoyt Bumbalough, Jerry's best friend, kept her promise and wrote every day.

Dear Maggie Sweet,

Jerry has taken a distant turn ever since you two have parted. Why, me and Hoyt hardly ever see him anymore. No doubt seeing us together reminds him how much he misses you. Any day now, I look for him to carry you back to Poplar Grove with a diamond on your third finger, left hand. It's only just a matter of time. You and Jerry are the cutest couple ever. (Except for Hoyt and me. Ha Ha.)

Maggie Sweet and Jerry   Mary Price and Hoyt
            Together 4-ever

                    Your best friend,
                        Mary Price Teeter

Her letters were so convincing I believed every word. I tried to stop brooding and told myself that soon, very soon, my dreams would come true. Jerry, my knight in shining armor, would rescue me in his Chevy, carry me back to Poplar Grove, and we'd live happily ever after.

Two long, lonely months went by without a word. By August, I was so full of longing and empty of pride, I broke down and wrote Jerry a love letter, scented with "To a Wild Rose" by Avon.

A few days later, Mary Price wrote that Jerry had married a girl named Brenda Faye Espy from Carrboro. The wedding, a shotgun affair, took place at the Court House, Saturday.

Mary Price added loyally, PS# 1 Jerry went off and joined the Navy. Good riddance to bad rubbish! He never was good enough for you anyway and everybody says the entire Espy family is nothing but pure-D-trash.

PS#2 I broke up with Hoyt too. Like I told him, anyone who could be best friends with someone as no-account as Jerry Roberts can't be worth shucks himself.

I did appreciate Mary Price's sacrifice of breaking up with Hoyt on my account, but when I got that letter I went all to pieces. I just couldn't believe the person I loved best in all the world had married someone else.

For four days, I stayed in the bed, played Elvis' "Are You Lonesome Tonight" and Patsy Cline's "Crazy" and cried my eyes out.

Poor Daddy didn't know what to do. He kept bringing me Goody's Headache Powders and cold cloths for my head. When that didn't work he tried Midol and the heating pad.

On the fourth day he threatened to call the doctor to come give me a nerve shot. That's when I pretended to feel better. Not because of doctors and needles, like Daddy thought, but because I could see I was scaring him and Willa Mae to death.

For the rest of the summer, I sulked around the house, took up smoking on the sly, and tried to avoid Daddy's worried eyes. When I wasn't working at the Tastee-Freeze, I stayed in my room, dressed in black, cried, and played the same sad records over and over again.

That whole long, lonely summer, all I thought about was Jerry. It was my fault he was married. My fault it was over between us. I'd broken up with him, then left town. He couldn't have known I still loved him. That it wasn't my choice to leave. If I hadn't broken up with him on prom night, if I hadn't always said no, maybe we'd be married and happy right now.

But outlaw boys never stayed with girls like me, I'd known that along. They married smart, fast girls like Brenda Faye.

Until that summer I'd always believed I was special, that I'd marry for love, do work that made me happy. Now life stretched out before me, flat and bleak, without Jerry or beauty school, without hope at all.

Then, late in August, I was coming up the hall from the back bedroom when I overheard Daddy and Willa Mae in the kitchen, talking about me.

Willa Mae said, "I swanee, Jack, Maggie Sweet doesn't seem the least bit excited over making a nurse."

Daddy said, "Well darlin', that's kindly my fault. You see, I was real tired that day. I meant to mark the beauty school box on the application form, but I accidentally marked the nursing school box instead. By the time I saw the mistake, it was too late to get my money back. But I didn't think she'd mind, her Mama being a nurse and all."

I froze. I couldn't believe what I was hearing.

Before I could move Willa Mae said, "Why, Jack Sweet, if that don't beat everything! You mean that child's been a'squallin' all summer 'cause she doesn't want to go to nurse's school?"

Before I could duck back in my room, I heard chair-legs scrape linoleum and Willa Mae met me in the hall. "Maggie Sweet, I think we need to have us a woman to woman talk. Your Daddy just told me you don't want to be a nurse a'tall."

I stood there paralyzed. This was important, but I didn't know what to do, what to say. Then I started bawling, "Oh, Willa Mae, all I ever wanted was to go to beauty school. Now that Jerry's gone, doing hair's my whole life."

"Well, Lord have mercy, child," she said, patting my arm, "I can't do nothing about that boy, but I swanee...your daddy thinking nursing school and beauty school are all the same...sometimes, I swear, that man just don't think."

A minute later, Willa Mae stomped out of the house. The next thing I heard was gravel flying, and the old pickup peeling down the driveway.

An hour later she was back. "It's all fixed, Maggie Sweet. You start beauty school Monday morning."

Chapter Three

Grandpa Pruitt had left Mama Dean. Mother had left Daddy. I figured that was the way of the world. People you loved broke your heart and the sun still came up like always, life went on, you grew up.

My troubles with Jerry had taken the shine off beauty school, but I figured if I had to be an old maid, at least I could have a job I loved. When I wasn't in school, I tried to stay too busy to think. I even volunteered as a candy-striper at the hospital on weekends. And even though I was only going through the motions, I was good at both jobs. Being raised in a boarding house had taught me how to *do* for people. (Why, Mother and Mama Dean would have skinned me alive if I hadn't known how to do.)

I'd been raised hearing: "Maggie Sweet, run upstairs and get Mama Dean's headache powders. She's getting one of her migraines."

"Miss Honeycutt got some bad news from home. Try to be extra sweet to her tonight."

"Maggie Sweet, don't put onion in Miss Skulock's salad. It'll talk back to her all day."

Also I didn't shock easy. Which is real important. I learned that doing hair.

Even when I was real young, I'd start brushing out someone's hair and pretty soon they'd start telling me things. They'd tell their life stories during a simple comb-out. And if I worked on them longer, like during a Toni or a Frost 'N Tip, they'd tell me things they wouldn't tell their own Mamas. They wouldn't have done that if I shocked easy.

Mostly, they just wanted to talk. But, sometimes they'd ask for advice. It's easy to know what's best for other people.

As a hospital candy-striper, folks told me everything. I guess it's easier to talk to a stranger. Also, my own heartache had given me more understanding. Sickness and love gone wrong are a lot the same. A heartache is a heartache no matter how it comes.

A lot of people couldn't see it that way, though. Miss Cato, the volunteer supervisor, thought I was real advanced. She was always saying things like, "Maggie, how did you know to hold that woman's hand in the emergency room today? We don't cover 'reassuring the patient' until spring."

I told her it was because I lived in a boarding house and did hair. She looked at me kind of funny, but one day she asked me to frost her hair and was barely in the chair before she started telling me all the problems she was having with her fiancé.

That year, I grew up a lot, made a perfect 4.00 in precision cutting and streaking. At night I practiced make-overs on Willa Mae, helped with supper and the dishes, and tried to forget my aching heart.

The following spring, while I was working at the hospital, Mr. Presson, my tenth grade biology teacher, was admitted to the hospital. He'd been visiting his mother in Chapel Hill for the weekend when he'd had an appendicitis attack. The attack was so bad he ended up having emergency surgery.

By the time I saw him, he was still pretty sick. And his bossy, stuck-up mother had aggravated the other volunteers 'til they all refused to go near his room. Naturally, they sent me. But I didn't mind. My heart went out to him. He was a bachelor, sick and alone in the world. Except for a mother who didn't like anyone, not even him.

After my shift was over, I took him magazines and books and he told me all the news from home. Before he left the hospital, he asked me to call him Steven.

When he was well enough to go home to Poplar Grove, I tried to get back to my old routine but I thought about Steven a lot.

Two weeks later, he called and asked me out. And just as calm as could be I said yes. It wasn't until after we hung up that I got nervous about what I'd tell Daddy and Willa Mae. I figured they'd have a pure fit what with Steven being so much older and all. (He was twenty-nine. I'd sneaked a look at his hospital chart.)

And they did get all fired-up. But not because of the age difference like I thought. It was because Steven was a college graduate. Daddy and Willa Mae had never had a college graduate in their house before.

It was the oddest thing! Daddy and Willa Mae spent the next two days cleaning that neat little mill house from top to bottom. They even painted the bathroom a shiny Pepto-Bismal pink color which was all the rage that year.

On the morning of my date, Daddy drove all the way into Chapel Hill to a bakery and bought a marble cake. He planned to serve the cake on cut-glass plates along with tiny little glasses of sherry. For some reason, Daddy thought marble cake from a bakery and sherry, all served on cut glass, was the height of refinement.

Up 'til then, I'd been calm as could be, but all this fussing had my nerves torn to pieces. At the last minute, I got so nervous I sneaked outside and smoked one of Daddy's Chesterfields behind a big rhododendron.

When Steven got there, I was in the bathroom gargling Listerine. Then everything fell into place. Steven put Daddy and Willa Mae at their ease and we picked up our conversation where we left off at the hospital.

When Steven told me he loved me after only one month, you could have knocked me over! I mean Steven was a grown *man*. Up 'til then, I'd only known boys who didn't have to shave every day. Why, I'd never expected a grown-up, college-educated man to feel *that way* about me.

For the next few months, Steven made the two-hour long trip to Chapel Hill every weekend. He was everything I thought an adult should be: steady and predictable, someone I could count on. Even his voice was calm and soothing. I liked that. I liked that his life had order. Everyone I knew seemed to barely get by from one minute to the next. But Steven had a plan, a life plan he was sure of. I thought if I could just study him long enough, I could learn to be that way too. I was tired of living off my emotions, tired of waiting around for my grown-up life to begin. So that July, when he asked me to marry him, I said I'd be honored. I even used that funny, old-timey word: honored. Because that was exactly how I felt.

Then, Steven did what I thought was the sweetest, most sincere thing. Before we told another living soul, he went to Daddy and asked for his blessing. Daddy was so thrilled over Steven's show of respect that he almost cried. I almost cried myself. ('Course now I know Steven only asked Daddy first because it was the proper thing to do.

Steven's very big on proper.)

That very same weekend, I took Steven back home to meet Mother and Mama Dean. Mother liked him right away, but Mama Dean gave him her all-men-are-only-after-one-thing-look. I held my breath and squeezed Steven's arm. Finally, she gave him her steeliest look and said, "Just what are your intentions towards our Maggie Sweet?"

"My intentions are honorable, ma'am," he said seriously.

"Do you work steady?" Her eyes glinted.

"Yes, ma'am. I'm a school teacher."

For a moment Mama Dean seemed to soften. Then came the question I had dreaded for weeks.

"And what church do you go to?"

The room went silent. All I could hear was the clock on the mantel strike, the motor in the refrigerator click on, and my heart pound so loud I was sure everyone heard it. My entire future hinged on how Mama Dean would take what Steven had to say next.

"Presbyterian, ma'am," he said, his voice firm.

"Well," she said, giving him a stern look. "A Presbyterian's just a Methodist with a college education."

When she smiled I knew that Steven had won her over. She even seemed to like him. This was amazing! Mama Dean had never liked anyone, man or woman, who wasn't a Methodist.

Later, Mother told me that after we left Mama Dean picked through the Whitman's Sampler Steven brought her and said absentmindedly, "That Steven's a man to go to the well with. Anyone who can't get along with him, couldn't get along with Jesus Christ."

After that, she considered Steven "kin" and was on his side no matter what.

In September, a week after I graduated from beauty school, we were married. It was a small Methodist church wedding with warm wishes from mine and Mary Price's family and the cold shoulder from Steven's side.

We were given a toaster, coffee-maker, linens and cash, and Steven gave me a beautiful add-a-pearl necklace.

After a short but wonderful honeymoon at Myrtle Beach we returned to Poplar Grove and I told Steven I couldn't wait to start working.

He gave me an odd look and said, "Maggie, marriage is a big adjustment. Wait a little while."

Nine months later our twin girls were born. They were prefect, adorable babies, with Steven's blonde hair and Mama Dean's Chinquapin-black eyes. We decided not to give them rhyming "twin" names, but called them Amy Elizabeth and Jill Carole. When Mama Dean heard the names she said, "Amy Elizabeth is right nice, but why in the world would anyone call a poor helpless baby Jill Kay-roley?" We told Mama Dean over and over again that it was not Jill Kay-roley, but Jill Carole—Carol with an E on the end of it. But no matter what we said she never got it right. But then, Mama Dean also called K-Mart "K-Mark," petites "petikes" and boys named Kevin "Calvin."

That same year we bought the old Shockley place on the corner of Morehead and Magnolia, three blocks from where I grew up. And even though the inside of the house was dark as a cave, I was tickled to death. It had a big garage out back—perfect for my Styles By Maggie shop.

We painted the house colonial blue, then filled it with flea market and family attic finds we refinished ourselves. We bought a couch and some beds. Mother Presson gave us a silver tea set, a *Gone With The Wind* lamp and a Queen Anne chair. Mother and Mama Dean gave us an antique hutch and the old brass bed Mama Dean was born in. I was thrilled. I'd been dreaming about how I'd decorate my very own house all my life. We'd tear out the dark mahogany paneling and paint and paper every room in warm, friendly cream and gold colors. I'd even make all the curtains on Mother's old Singer treadle. When we were through, everything would be as warm and cheerful as a page out of Sears-Roebuck catalog.

But Steven said, "Maggie Sweet, I know you've never had much and you've got a lot to learn. but, that's genuine mahogany paneling. We *don't tear out genuine mahogany paneling*." He said each word slow and drawn-out, like he thought I was backward or something.

When I asked for sheer curtains to let in some light, Steven hung heavy wine-colored velvet drapes at every window, then covered the walls with dark, gloomy portraits of his long-dead relatives hung from guy wires attached to the ceiling molding (so the nail-holes wouldn't "disfigure" his precious paneling).

I remember looking around the house, *my* house, and thinking, Lord have mercy, this place is as creepy as a museum and this man's a stranger. But, then I'd cuddle my sweet, dark-eyed babies and think, grow up, Maggie Sweet. You're not a child anymore; you're twenty years old with children of your own. Even if this isn't the way you thought it would be, he's a good man. You can do this. You can be whatever it is he wants you to be.

So, we joined Steven's church and a neighborhood improvement group, and we went to all the school functions. Steven joined the Historical Society, the Sons of the Confederacy, and a Presbyterian Men's group. I missed cutting hair like crazy, so I read all the hairstyle magazines and practiced on friends and family. (During the day when

Steven wasn't at home. He had hissy fits over what he called "women traipsing through the house.")

I also volunteered at the hospital and the Methodist home and stayed so busy, I barely had time to shave both legs on the same day.

Then, things settled down. By the time the girls were ready for first grade we were so settled that the only thing that ever changed was the display of magazines on the front room coffee table.

That September I asked Steven what he thought about me finally starting to work.

He said, "Wait until the girls are a little bigger."

So I waited and became Maggie Sweet, Homeroom Mother and Queen of the Kitchen Sink, while Steven went on for his master's degree and locked himself in the den the nights he was at home.

I'd visit Mother, Mama Dean, and Mary Price. Every chance I got, I'd sneak down to Shirley's and breathe in the scent of Matrix shampoo and Zoto permanents. When I got home, I'd read the fine print on my cosmetology license, and even if I had to use my birthday money from Daddy, I kept my license renewed.

By the time the girls were in junior high and bigger than me, I told Steven that I thought I'd waited long enough.

This time he didn't say anything. He just stood there looking like I had slapped him. Then, he slammed into the den and tore the Poplar Grove phone book half-in-two.

After that, my life became as predictable as our meals. I raised the girls, cooked and cleaned. Six times a year, I served chicken a-la-king at banquets where the topics were fund-raising or tombstone-rubbing. Every quarter, we changed the furnace filter, and Steven's mother came to visit. On our wedding anniversary, I put on a shirtwaist dress, low-heels and the add-a-pearl necklace and Steven took me out for a forty-five minute dinner at the K & W Cafeteria. We made love every Saturday night, right after the eleven o'clock news. Sunday morning, right after church, Steven updated the magazines on the coffee table, and raked the rug 'til all our footprints disappeared.

It wasn't until my coffee got cold and the sun came up that I realized I'd been rocking in the glider, thinking things over, for hours. I jerked myself back to reality. *You're not Maggie Sweet anymore. You're Maggie Sweet Presson. Steven's wife. The mother of two almost grown girls.* In another half hour or so the alarm clock would go off, my family would awake and start flipping on light switches, getting ready for their day. But I wasn't ready to go inside yet. I still had some thinking to do. For years, Steven had slammed the door on my beauty shop dreams and I'd shoved it to the back of my mind. I'd shoved *everything* to the back of my mind until Steven spent our savings on cemetery plots and I started to see how much time had passed. I sat under the magnolia, watching the sun rise, thinking about my class reunion and Jerry; thinking about my life. Now I wondered if all these things hadn't happened at the same time, would I have even noticed that I'd spent all these years sleep-walking.

I felt my life take a turn, a hard bump.

Chapter Four

Horoscope for April—Poplar Grove Expositor

Balance introspection with fun. If your social life seems meager, do something about it. Refuse to be swayed by one who shouts invectives. Someone important will enter your life at precisely the right moment.

It rained all week, a real gullywasher that seemed to go on forever. All week, I sighed, stared out the window and picked the dead leaves off the African violets on the kitchen window sill. On Friday, I noticed that I'd picked every last leaf off one of the violets and thought, Good Lord, Maggie, get a hold of yourself. You've killed that poor flower dead as a hammer.

Monday morning, Modine Dingler, a former classmate, called to invite me to an Around-the-World Home Lingerie Party at her house Wednesday night.

I'd sworn off house parties years before (I had enough Tupperware to sink Coxey's Navy). But when Modine said a lot of our old classmates would be there, I promised to call her back.

Then, Tuesday, something happened that told me I

had to go to Modine's party or die.

I was carrying a basket of clean, folded laundry past the den, when I overheard Steven on the phone. "Don't worry about a thing, Theo. We'll have the meeting here Wednesday night."

Theodora Bloodworth is president of the local historical society. She and Steven are on *beaucoup* committees together. If you saw Theo anywhere you'd know right off, historical-society president. She's forty-something, lives in a big old turreted house on West Main, has a plantation accent saying *chay-ah* for chair and *cen-tah* for center. Theo wears cameo brooches, clothes edged in silk ribbon, and her hair in a chignon like the late Princess Grace.

Now Steven was saying, "Theo, I insist. You already work too hard and good, old reliable Maggie doesn't have anything else to do."

I stopped dead in my tracks, my face burning. "Good, old, reliable Maggie doesn't have anything else to do!" I think I said the words out loud. When had I been reduced to 'good, old reliable, Maggie?'

Suddenly the laundry basket felt like it was filled with rocks. I carried it upstairs, put everything away, then went back to the kitchen to wash supper dishes.

By the time the sink was filled with hot, sudsy water, I was filled with rage. 'Good, old reliable Maggie doesn't have anything else to do!' What an awful thing to say! It wasn't even true. I had plenty to do. It was just that no one would let me do it.

Then this feeling of unbearable longing came over me and tears stung my eyes. It was true. I *didn't* have anything else to do. Nothing important anyway. I'd spent all my life waiting around for Steven or someone else to give me permission to start living my real life.

A few minutes later, when Steven strolled into the kitchen, I was scrubbing the creamed-potato pan with an SOS pad. He poured himself a cup of coffee and said, "We're having the meeting here Wednesday night. I need you to do the usual—serve cake and coffee, take minutes."

I kept scrubbing away, not saying a word. I wanted to say, I'd rather take poison that do that! Finally, I said, "Steven Presson, it might surprise you to know that I've got my own plans Wednesday night."

He stared at me over the tops of his half-glasses. "What are you doing that's so important?"

"I'm seeing some friends!"

"Well, Maggie, this is a fine time to tell me. This meeting's important. You can see your friends any time."

This was getting worse and worse. I turned the water on full-force and clanged the pans together as much as possible, hoping if I ignored him, he'd go away. But he just stood there, rolling his eyes, giving me his, "Lord-give-me-patience-with-fools-and-Maggie" look.

I turned off the water and slung the pan into the dish drainer. "Look, Steven, you had no right to volunteer me! No right at all! You can make the coffee and serve the cake. Maybe poor overworked Theo will take the minutes! 'Good, old reliable Maggie' won't be here!"

Steven just looked at me. Finally he said, "For heaven's sake, Maggie. Sometimes I wonder about you. You get so worked up over nothing." Then he sighed real big, like I'd let him down once again, and stomped back to the den.

The minute the den door shut, I felt like a hundred pound weight landed on me. Why had I made such a fuss? I didn't even want to go to Modine's party. Maybe I did get worked up over nothing. Maybe I owed it to Steven. I started toward the den to apologize, to tell him I'd changed my mind about helping. Then I remembered, 'good, old, reliable Maggie.' I stood stock still. I was *always* changing my plans to suit everyone and what did I get for my trouble? "Good, old, reliable" was what I got.

Well, it was time to sink or swim, fish or cut bait, drop the coin or get off the bus. Only a fool or plueperfect martyr would work for the title 'good, old, reliable.'

An Around-The-World-Lingerie party seemed like an odd place to start. But I had to start somewhere. At least Modine's party was *my* choice, and I wouldn't be serving coffee and cake to the likes of Steven and Theo Bloodworth.

By Wednesday, I was looking forward to the party. I was only sorry Mary Price couldn't go. With her singing at the That'lldu Bar & Grill and all, she's just busy all the time. She made me promise to call her later and tell her all about the party, which I planned to do anyway.

All that day, I caught myself wondering what people did at lingerie parties. In my mind, I pictured row upon row of underwear displayed like shiny, pastel, see-through Tupperware, on a big table in Modine's front room.

While I dressed, (I planned to wear my beige church-dress, but it went all to pieces in the washer so I had to wear my navy dotted-swiss even though it was pushing the season) I wondered if Modine would make her husband, Ellis, keep the children out of the house for the entire evening, the theme of the party being underwear and all.

Right after supper, I set the dining room table with a linen tablecloth, the silver tea set, and a chocolate chess pie. Then I left the house early to avoid Steven's "how-could-you-do-this-to me?" look.

Driving down East Main to Townsend Avenue, I passed the city limits sign, the That'lldu Bar and Grill where Mary Price and Hoyt sing on weekends, the farmer's market, then under a bridge spray painted with the warning "Jesus or Hell." Within seconds, there were rolling fields dotted with wild azalea, bluebonnets, buttercups and clover. Cattle grazed on the hillsides. I rolled down the car window and took a deep breath. The air was thick and sweet. I could feel it on my skin. A minute later, I bypassed Modine's old farm house, a stand of loblolly pines, Belews Pond, then, on impulse, I circled back to Chatham Road— Jerry's old home place.

The house needed painting—had always needed painting. But I'd always loved it. It was a small Victorian, with a wide, sunny side porch, an open gazebo-like turret, yellow and purple stained-glass windows, all on a couple of acres of land.

I hadn't been here for years, but back when the girls were little and I first knew I'd married a stranger, I rode out to Chatham Road a few times. Then one day, I stopped. Jerry was gone. It was time to forget him. I was married to Steven. My life was decided.

Now, I inched into the dirt driveway, ready to back out at any signs of life. But the house looked deserted: the curtains were closed, the porch furniture was gone and the grass was mowed in a careless, chewed-off way of a neighbor trying to keep it from getting snaky-looking.

I wondered if Jerry's folks had sold the old place when they'd retired. I wondered where they were now, where Jerry was now, but most of all I wondered why I'd come here after all this time.

Memories washed over me, memories of summer nights parked at Belews Pond. The crickets chirping in the tall grass, the air heavy with the scent of honeysuckle and Jerry's Canoe aftershave, his melting blue eyes and the catch in his voice as he sang "Chances Are" along with Johnny Mathis on the car radio.

I sat there for a while, maybe five minutes. Then, heaving a sigh for good things past, I made my mind go blank and circled back to Modine's.

By the time I got there there were half a dozen cars in the driveway: Doris Binfield's old green station wagon, Geneva Cantrow's blue Dodge Dart, Jessie Rae Moore's white Honda Civic and Dreama Nim's Ford with the I B 4 JESUS-WHO U B 4 bumper sticker.

For some reason, Dreama answered the door. She was wearing her usual polyester muumuu, bubble-gum pink lipstick (even on her teeth) and her hair was piled up so high she was in danger of the ceiling fans.

I had just joined the others in the front room, when suddenly Modine shouted, "That's a pure lie, Doris! Toy Overcash is the best wife and mother I know."

(Doris Binfield is the choir director's wife. She and Modine have been best friends for years. I just wish you could have seen the hurt look on Doris' face when Modine called her a liar!)

Jessie Rae Moore, who is pretty as a picture but so quiet, I used to think she was backward, started crying. "I know! I know!" she said, so broken-up I could hardly understand her. "But it's the Lord's truth. She's gone. Bag and baggage."

"What...?" I said. But they were too upset to hear me.

"Well, I won't believe it. I *won't* believe it! There must have been foul play," Modine said.

"No...she left a note," Doris said. She was fanning

herself with a mint green nightie from the lingerie display. All the color had left her face and she looked like she was about to faint.

Dreama just stood there smirking all over herself. She was dying to tell me the whole story but I wouldn't give her the satisfaction of asking her personally.

"What's going on?" I asked again. But everyone was too wrought up to hear me.

"The note said: 'I just can't take it anymore,'" Geneva said, and her chin began quivering and she started to cry too.

Now I was all shook up. *"Can't take what anymore?"* I shouted. By the way everyone's heads whipped around I could tell I'd said this way too loud.

"Oh, Maggie Sweet." Dreama said, "You don't know, do you darlin'? Toy Overcash left. Just like that," and she snapped her fingers to show me how it was. "She just said, 'I can't take it anymore,' and walked out on Bobby and the kids."

Well, I like to have had a dying duck fit! The blood in my ears roared so loud I couldn't hear anything else. It just couldn't be true! If ever there was a town-good-woman, Toy Overcash was it. She'd spent her whole life teaching Sunday school, volunteering at the Methodist Home and sending recipes to the Pillsbury bake-off. (If she won she planned to give the prize money to the homeless. Even Mary Price says that next to the word "good" in the dictionary, they could just show a picture of Toy Overcash. "Good" wouldn't need any other definition. 'Course, Mary Price, being who she is, laughed when she said it. But it was true.)

I thought back to last year, when Miss Skurlock, my old homeroom teacher and one of Mama Dean's boarders, died. Toy got there right behind the ambulance. By the time Mother and I got back to the house, she had Mama Dean settled and was organizing the wake. Why, she cooked and vacuumed through the entire tragedy.

Toy Overcash was a rock. She'd helped everyone in this town. She was the one person we could count on, no matter what. If she could walk out on her family, nothing in this world was sacred!

Well, after that news, it took a long time for the party to settle down. Modine apologized to Doris for calling her a liar, and they both cried several times. Doris was still hurt, but she said she knew it was just the shock of it all. And we all knew that Dreama stirred things up even more.

Later, we tried to go on with the party since Modine had gone to the trouble of making up all those little ham biscuits, a lime-green passion fruit punch, and her special coconut cake. But it just wasn't the same. No one's mind was on food or lingerie anymore.

Right after we ate, everyone placed their orders and we all went home. I bought a discontinued sample with some grocery money I had stuck back and got to take mine home with me.

When I got home, I was still so worked up that even before I called Mary Price, I went directly to the freezer in the basement and pulled out the Sucrets Throat Lozenges tin, hidden clear in the back underneath the frozen zucchini.

Last year, when I quit smoking, I'd put four Marlboro Lights in a Sucrets tin in case of an emergency. I had to put the cigarettes in kind of kaddy-corner, otherwise they just wouldn't go. Then I wrapped the tin in foil, put it all in a zip-lock bag and hid it under the zucchini.

It was like I knew that some day my life would be nothing but one big crisis right after another.

Frozen cigarettes light as good as the regular kind. I'd wondered about that. I smoked one of the cigarettes right down to the filter. Then I wrapped up the three that were left, put them back in the tin, and went upstairs to call Mary Price.

We talked until real late about what we could do to help Bobby Overcash and the children. Their situation wasn't exactly covered in Emily Post. Finally, around midnight, we decided that people have to eat, no matter what.

But that night, I had the awfullest nightmare. I dreamed the sourdough rising in the Overcash refrigerator went completely crazy. You have to feed sourdough or it dies, it's a living thing.

In my dream, the day Toy left, she packed her bags, put a chicken in the crock pot for her family's supper, then on the way out the door she remembered to feed the sourdough.

All I can figure, the state Toy was in, she fed the sourdough too much. So the minute she went out the back door it began pulsing and writhing. It made this sound like a little tiny heartbeat! By the middle of the night that heartbeat was so loud you could hear it clear in the next room. But the family, sleeping innocently in their beds upstairs, never heard a thing.

Before long, that sourdough had doubled, and tripled, and quadrupled in size 'til it blew the door slam off the refrigerator! Then it really took off growing. By now the whole house reeked with yeasty smell of warm sourdough gone rampant.

In just a few minutes it filled up the entire first floor! Then before you could say Jack Robinson, it started oozing up the stairs to where Bobby Overcash and the children were fast asleep. And without any warning whatsoever, Bobby Overcash and the four Overcash children were completely overcome!

That's how Toy found them when she came home the next morning after thinking things over. In the short time she was gone her entire family had drowned in their sleep in a sticky, writhing mass of uncooked bread!

That's when I sat up straight in bed in a cold sweat!

I was wide awake for a long time thinking about Toy and Bobby. They'd seemed like a perfect couple. I wondered if they'd had one big fight or if they'd just drifted apart over the years.

Everyone thought Steven and I were perfect too.

Suddenly this feeling of utter doom came over me and I felt like the loneliest person in the world.

Steven, who was sound asleep next to me, must have sensed something because even in his sleep he mumbled, "Maggie Sweet, are you all right?"

For some reason, this set me off and I started crying. I guess it was the unexpected kindness of it. When he rolled over to his side of the bed, I reached for his hand but it was wedged tight under his pillow. So I stretched out my foot and found his tangled up in the sheet.

The last thing I remember, as I drifted off to sleep, was my foot resting against Steven's and what a comfort it was.

Chapter Five

Thursday morning, Mary Price picked me up in her Silverado and we drove to the Overcash's with our dishes. I took a chicken rice casserole and Mary Price took a store-bought pecan pie.

But when we pulled up in front of the Overcash house, there in the driveway, big as life, was Toy's red Volkswagen!

"Lord, she's back! Don't stop!" I shouted.

Mary Price threw the Silverado into gear, hit the gas pedal, and kept on going.

"That story about her leaving's probably a bold-faced lie from beginning to end," Mary Price said. "Nobody runs away for just one night."

I thought about all the times Mary Price had left Hoyt for an hour, or a night, or however long it took to get her way, but I didn't say anything. We just drove around the block trying to figure out what to do. Then I noticed the car in front of us was circling the block, too.

"Why, that's Geneva Cantrow's Dodge Dart!" I said.

She'd been circling the block about as long as we had.

Mary Price looked in the rear view mirror. "Lord, Maggie Sweet, that's Doris Binfield's old green station wagon following us! Why, every good woman in town has turned out."

(Mary Price has a morbid fear of being seen with "gaggles of good women." She says, "Those high-pitched voices trying to out-nice each other make me want to scream and claw my eyes out!")

Next to Doris, in the passenger seat, was Modine Dingler. And behind them, Jessie Rae Moore's Honda Civic. All the women from last night's party were driving past the Overcash house, then circling the block.

Finally, we all pulled over at a stop sign and got out of our cars. Everyone agreed it would be real awkward for us to bust in on Toy and Bobby if they were trying to iron things out. We decided to go for coffee at Eckerd's and talk things over.

(I decided not to say anything about my sourdough dream, even though the Overcash house was as quiet as a tomb. I figured everyone was already upset enough.)

When we got to Eckerd's, we found a booth in the back. After about three cups of coffee apiece, we decided that since Geneva's husband, Knoxie, and Bobby Overcash are co-managers down at Winn-Dixie, she'd be the first to hear. Geneva promised to call the rest of us the minute she heard anything.

Modine had baked two lemon-chess pies. Doris had a green bean casserole. Geneva had half a honey-baked ham and Jessie Rae had this orange-congealed-salad that hadn't quite jelled. But we all knew Jessie Rae had really tried so we divided everything up equally and went home.

After Mary Price dropped me off, I was too worked up to do any housework. I just sat in the front room in Steven's La-Z-Boy trying to figure things out.

I thought about Toy and Bobby together again; how she'd been the perfect wife right up to the moment she walked out the door. Now she'd have to spend the rest of her life making up to Bobby for one mistake. I thought how awful that would be.

Then I remembered how sweet Steven had been last night, comforting me like that. So far nothing had happened between us but a little boredom. Maybe if I quit worrying about how boring my life was, I could think up something to add some excitement to our marriage before things got worse. Once we were getting along better, I could explain to Steven just what he was doing wrong.

I had to try, I mean, you don't throw away a nineteen year old marriage and a house in the historical part of town because of a little boredom.

The rest of the afternoon, I sat in the La-Z-Boy thinking and reading back copies of "Can This Marriage Be Saved" in the *Ladies Home Journal*.

Just before my family got home, I came up with an idea.

Right after supper, when Steven went into his den, as usual, I sent the children over to Mother's. I told them she needed help with her yard work—which wasn't exactly a lie, even though Mother had never *asked* for help.

Then I poured Steven's favorite wine into our best glasses. The wine tasted like Alka-Seltzer to me, but our marriage was worth the sacrifice.

I took a sip of the wine, then carried both glasses upstairs to the bedroom and arranged them just so on the night stand.

When I turned on the radio, Elvis was singing, "I Can't Help Falling In Love With You." I figured that was a sign.

I took another sip of the wine.

After I showered, I painted up and slipped into the

black silk teddy I'd bought at the lingerie party. I'd never seen a teddy before. It's a lot like shorty pajamas, only sexy. I figured me buying that teddy was another sign that I was doing the right thing.

I tried another sip of the wine, which was starting to grow on me. After that, I splashed on some Jean Naté and called Steven up to the bedroom.

The radio played "Love Is A Many Splendored Thing" as Steven came up the stairs. I stood, stark naked except for the teddy and tiniest spray of Naté, waiting for my whole new life to begin.

Well, I wish you could have seen the look on Steven's face when he came through the bedroom door. He just stood there in the doorway staring at me, his eyes all bugged out, his jaw dropped down to the floor and his face dead white. I have never seen a man look so surprised in all my life. Then, all at once his face went red. But not like he was blushing. More like he was about to have a stroke.

Finally he said, and I will never forget his words, "Maggie Sweet, what in the world has come over you? You know I have a Sons of the Confederacy meeting tonight. Besides, it's only Thursday."

Well, I *did* know he had a meeting. I just didn't think he'd care about an old meeting with what I had on my mind. I said, "Steven, do you love me? I need to know if you still love me."

Steven just looked at me. "I married you, didn't I? What more do you want?"

After he left, I sat down on the bed and had a good cry. If you have ever stood stark naked except for a teddy, in front of the person who's been begging you to do that very thing for years, and he doesn't want you, then you know what I mean.

After awhile I gathered myself as best I could and packed the teddy away. Then, I carried the wine out to the glider and drank until dark.

This is what I hope I can forget some day.

Chapter Six

Friday morning, I was lower than a well. I'd been a fool to think a black silk teddy could change anything: make Steven notice me, make things better between us. Nothing was ever going to change. Steven wanted a quiet little woman, one who'd stay in the background, run his house, raise his children, and do it all so smoothly he could put her completely out of his mind.

But I didn't want to be quiet anymore. I wanted to make a fuss, to shout, "It's not enough!" Only somewhere along the way I'd lost him, lost the power to make him see or hear me.

One of Steven's pet rules is about television watching. No one is allowed to turn on the TV 'til after supper. No exceptions. Not ever. He says there are a million and one things a person can do instead of wasting their life away watching TV. So that Friday, I planned to watch TV from "Good Morning America" right through to "The Five O'clock News."

I was just getting settled when the telephone rang. It was Mary Price.

"What're you doing?"

"Cussing, smoking and watching TV."

"Whoa! A walk on the wild side! What's up?"

"Nothing. Nothing but Toy and Bobby. Steven and me. Nothing but life."

"Lord, Maggie Sweet, life's too big a subject to think about in the morning! I don't mean to add to your burden, but I need you pin up the hem on a new costume I got for this weekend's gig."

Mary Price rehearses at the That'lldu nearly every day. She and Hoyt have been singing country music there for about a year. The That'lldu is a real dump and only no-accounts go in there. But Mary Price says, "A person has to start her singing career someplace."

"Try to come around one o'clock," I said. "I'm fixing to watch TV all day and I don't think I can live through the soap operas. I mean, all those couples having meaningful talks and making love right through kidnappings, killings and amnesia...why, a Sons of the Confederacy meeting wouldn't slow them down a heartbeat."

"You'll go into a total decline watching soaps in your mood. You need to get busy. Go down to the Curl & Swirl...watch Shirley work...shampoo a few people...throw yourself into hair. It's therapy for you."

"I know. But, Shirley's at a style show in Atlanta. She won't be home 'til tomorrow. Besides, her shop's dead as four o'clock since the Beauty Box opened at the mall with its air guns, blending shears, and vent dryers."

"But Shirley's always had the busiest shop in town!"

"Well, now its the second busiest and there aren't but two shops."

"Go to the Beauty Box. Watch them cut hair. All those high-tech precision cuts! Weren't precision cuts your specialty back in school?"

"I got straight As. But, that was back when God was a boy."

"It hasn't been that long! Why, you could pick it up again in a heartbeat, start cutting hair at home..."

"Nobody wants their hair done at the kitchen sink, Mary Price. It's too awkward. I need chairs that tilt, shampoo basins..."

"You need your own shop."

"Steven'll never allow that. Beauty shops don't go with historical."

"It's a wonder he doesn't have you dressing like 'Little House on the Prarie' and churning your own butter."

"I know," I said, feeling low again. "I'd love to watch a good precision hair-cutter. I'm getting so rusty. It's just...I'd feel disloyal to Shirley setting foot in the Beauty Box. Poor Shirley. Big hair and tight perms are dead as a hammer and that's all she knows."

"Well, go to Eckerd's and check out the new hair products! Do something!"

"I was supposed to do Jessie Rae's hair today, but she canceled for the millionth time."

"You do Jessie Rae's hair?"

"Sad to say but I do."

"I love Jessie Rae to death but she hasn't changed her hairdo since 1979. And those roots..."

"I know. I keep trying to talk her into a change but she's too timid to change anything, even her hair. It's been six months since I talked her into a little #104 Natural golden brown hair color. Then, her family pitched a fit and she hasn't been back. All that premature gray and no touch-ups...why, she's got more roots than Alex Haley!"

"From the back it looks like a bald spot!" Mary Price said.

"If she had a streaking or a reverse frosting she wouldn't get roots every little whipstitch," I said.

"She'll do that when hogs fly."

"I've been trying to talk her into a shorter cut with

full bangs. It'd bring out her eyes."

"Lord, Maggie, she'll be wearing that teased-up-bubble hairdo to the old-folks home. But, I gotta go now. See you at one."

After we talked I felt better. I turned off the TV, straightened the house, then carried my sewing kit downstairs so I'd be ready when Mary Price arrived with her costume. I was only pinning up a hem, but Mary Price traipsing all over town in her wild cowgirl outfits aggravated Steven to death so it tickled me to know I was in on it.

I managed to stay busy and before I knew it it was lunch time.

I was in the kitchen fixing a peanut butter and mayonnaise sandwich when the menu on the side of the refrigerator caught my eye.

The menu is Steven's latest attempt to land me in the quiet room at Broughten Mental Hospital.

Every month he makes up a menu of what we'll be eating morning, noon and night for the next thirty days. There's no discussing it—it's chiseled in stone like the Ten Commandments.

First he inventories every speck of leftovers in the house to see what we have to work with. (It's a wonder he didn't find the Marlboros tucked behind the frozen zucchini!) Then he'll spend hours studying grocery ads and clipping coupons. The only foods he considers are double-coupon food and two-for-one food.

And he's as tight as Dick's hatband with leftovers. Why, if you get carried away enjoying Sunday's roast, you'll eat meatless hash later in the week 'cause every ounce of that roast is rationed out for other meals. (You won't like meatless hash one bit, either. I know.)

Being raised in a boarding house had taught me to

cut corners. But the way Steven went about it was enough to make a preacher cuss. Like last month, when we were shopping at Winn-Dixie, I picked up a bottle of ginger ale for this Celestial Golden Salad we all like. (The one with oranges in it.) But when I carried the ginger ale to the check-out, Steven told me to put it back. *To put it back*, mind you, right there are the check-out, in front of everybody. Because it wasn't on special.

Well, this flew all over me. So I plunked six quarters on the counter, to pay for the ginger ale, and prissed my tail right out of the store, leaving Steven to carry everything.

That's when I decided to never shop with Steven again. But then I started thinking that'd probably suit him just fine and I wouldn't have any say at all.

I was still in the kitchen going over the menu when Mary Price knocked on the back door. She was dressed in a red tube top, tight jeans and cowgirl boots. Also, she was carrying a Coke. Mary Price never goes anywhere without a Coke. Just seeing her made me feel better.

But when I let her in, I noticed that her eyes were big as plates, and underneath the pancake make up, she was white as flour.

"Mary Price, what in the world...?"

"The beatingest thing has happened!" She slid into a chair and fanned herself with a paper napkin like she was having a sinking spell. "I've just had the shock of my life! Let me catch my breath and I'll tell you."

She lit a Virginia Slim and offered me one. I got up, closed the back door and all the curtains, and took it. If Mary Price was this shook up, I'd need all the help I could get.

Finally, she took a deep ragged breath and started. "I just come from the That'lldu. Bobby Overcash's brother Jimmy was in there."

"Did you ask about Toy?"

"Do fat babies fart? Of course I asked! Jimmy said Toy had run off all right, to West Virginia..."

"West Virginia! Why, she won't hardly drive to Charlotte. She's scared of interstates."

"Interstates?"

"Interstates and regular highways, too."

"Well, she called Bobby from Parkersburg and told him she'd left him and wasn't ever coming home unless he met her conditions."

"Conditions? What do you mean?"

"She told Bobby he'd been having a middle-age crisis ever since she met him. Now she was fixin' to have a crisis of her own. First off, she said, he wasn't to call her Toy anymore, but Tamara. Bobby said he thought Toy was right cute, but if that's what she wanted she could consider it done. Then she said he couldn't go on any hunting or fishing trips till she had the money to go back to school."

"Wait a minute! Toy did go to school. She graduated with us. Anyway when did Bobby take up hunting and fishing?"

"Lord, Maggie Sweet. You *have* been home too long. Why, Bobby's always done anything he takes a notion to do. Toy's wanted to go to art school for years, but every time she saved the money Bobby'd take a spell and spend it on fishing trips, hunting trips, at the That'lldu..."

"But, I always thought they were perfect!"

"Shoot! The only thing they ever agreed on is that they were both in love with Bobby Overcash."

"I can't believe it...Toy is good at art, though.

Remember her Coke-bottle stained glass back in school? And the cartoon pictures she made at the Lions Club barbecue?"

"Caricatures."

"What?"

"Those cartoon pictures are called caricatures. Most caricatures make people look deformed but Toy's were right cute. But when she mentioned art school, Bobby pitched a fit, said she was a wife and mother now and it was time for her to grow up."

"Lord, and her with a heart of gold. What happened then?"

Mary Price paused, put out her cigarette and lit another one. "That's when she hung up on him!"

"She what?"

"She hung up. She gave him time to remember that she was 300 miles from home, that the kids would be up in a few hours, and that he didn't even know where they kept the pots and pans."

"That'd be my family. They don't know where anything is."

"When she called back he said he thought art school was a good idea. But that wasn't enough for Toy. Not only did she want to go to school but he had to build her an art studio in the garage—and when he came in later'n ten o'clock he could cook his own damned supper 'cause she'd be busy in her studio."

"Did she really say 'damned'? Toy never cusses."

"I reckon she did. That's when Bobby should have known she meant business. But her cussing went right over his head. So the fool said, 'That's not one condition, Toy, that's three. And who said anything about a' art studio?' And furthermore, Toy Overcash, don't you ever, ever, hang up on me again.'"

"What'd she do then?"

"Hung up of course! She had to. She'd come too far to back down. By the time she called back, Bobby Overcash was a broken man. He agreed to everything and she went home."

"Mary Price, I am shocked in my heart. Do you really think she'd have stayed gone?"

"That's the thing. I don't know what to think. I can't believe she went off in the first place. I mean Toy's always been so mealy-mouthed...like that woman in 'Gone With The Wind'."

"Melanie Wilkes."

"Who?"

"Melanie—the woman in 'Gone With The Wind.' Toy makes Melanie look like a painted hussy."

"Jimmy said she'd been changing...watching Phil Donahue, saying things like 'self-actualization' and 'down with oppression.' 'Course Bobby didn't know what any of that meant. He did think it was strange when she started wearing blue eye-shadow in the day and her hair in a long braid like Willie Nelson."

We sat there for the longest, not saying a word. After we took a last drag on our cigarettes, we stubbed them out, and I washed the ashtray and sprayed the room with Lysol.

Finally, Mary Price said, "All these years I thought Toy was a little nothing of a woman, but she has the guts of Atilla the Hun! Maggie, do you think she was just pretending to be sweet all those years? I never trusted anyone *that* sweet. It's not natural. Why, she completely blindsided Bobby. She blindsided the whole town."

After Mary Price left, I didn't hardly have the sense to cook. All I could think about was Toy. But by the time supper was on the stove, I'd decided that Toy hadn't blindsided anyone. Not on purpose, anyway. She didn't have a mean, sneaky bone in her body. She was a good woman. That's what had been her undoing. She'd spent her whole life helping everyone, and we'd all let her help us. But when she needed help, no one said, "Now it's your turn Toy. You tell us what you need and we'll help you."

She ran away because she was worn out with being good.

I was still deep in thought when my family sat down for supper.

Right off, Jill said, "God, Mama. I'm sick of butter beans. Why do we always have to have butter beans? Week in, week out, it's butter beans, butter beans."

I wanted to say, Please don't fuss. I'm too upset to listen to fussing tonight. Besides it's on the menu to have butter beans week in and week out and your Daddy sets great store by his menus. What I said is, "Jill, watch your cussing."

"I don't want to speak to you again about your cussing," Steven said, not looking up from his plate.

"Why is the meatloaf so bready? I hate bready meatloaf," Amy said.

Naturally, it's bready when it's mostly bread. Your Daddy only allows me three-quarters of a pound of hamburger for meatloaf for four people so he can buy *important* things like cemetery plots, is what I was thinking. "The starving people in the world would be thrilled to have this meatloaf," is what I said.

"Well, I'd rather have one skinny hamburger than a huge slab of bready old meatloaf any day of the week," Amy said, looking down her nose at me.

"Maggie, are you sure tonight's meatloaf night? I thought it was fish stick night."

"No, Steven. Every *other* Friday's fish stick night." We'd had this conversation so many times, I wanted to put my head in the ice tea pitcher and drown myself.

Steven got up from the table, went out to the kitchen and checked the menu. When he returned he said. "Hmm, I could have sworn it was fish stick night. Oh, well, eat your meatloaf, Amy."

"Well, then, pass the ketchup, *please*," she said.

"Jill," Steven said, "what on earth's wrong with your ears?"

For the first time I noticed there were plastic strings hanging from Jill's ears.

"Nothing's wrong. I got my ears double-pierced. I have to wear nylon fishing line in the holes 'til they heal. If I wear earrings too soon, I'll end up with running sores for earlobes," Jill said.

"That's disgusting," Amy said.

"Do we have to discuss infection at the table?" Steven said.

"But, Daddy, you asked..."

"I also told you over and over again that you weren't allowed to get your ears double-pierced."

"God, Daddy, you're so old-fashioned. All of my friends..."

"I don't care about your friends." Steven said.

"Her friends are nothing but pure trash," Amy sniffed.

"At least I have friends." Jill said.

"It's a pity none of them are human!" Amy said.

"Shut up."

"You shut up."

"Jill, when I tell you something, I mean for you to listen. By, the way, have you sent those college applications off like I told you? It's April and you've already been turned down by eight schools," Steven said.

"I told you I ain't going. I'm sick of school. I can't stand the thoughts of four more years," Jill said.

"If you don't go to college, I'm signing you up for computer school. You can work in a bank or an office. And don't say 'ain't.' Only low class people say 'ain't,'" Steven said.

"Well, if that makes me low class, I guess I'm low class," Jill said.

"You're not low class. You're anything but low class," I said.

Amy smirked, but I glared at her and she didn't say anything.

"Not everyone's cut out for college. Mama never went," Jill said.

"Well, that's some recommendation," Steven said.

"Thanks a lot, Steven," I said.

"I didn't mean it that way. You know I didn't mean it that way. I just meant...I'm paying her way through college and you'd think I'd insulted her. Why does she have to act so contrary—so odd." Steven's face was getting red.

"She's not *acting* odd. She *is* odd," Amy said.

"Everyone's odd one way or another. There's no law against being odd in my book," I said.

"Thanks a lot, Mama," Jill snapped.

"This subject is closed," Steven bellowed. "Tomorrow you *will* send those applications and I don't want to hear another word about it. Now, Amy, pass the ketchup."

Amy passed the ketchup.

Everyone stared at their plates. There was about a pound of ketchup on each plate. The meatloaf, potato pancakes, and butter beans were all swimming in ketchup. We used a ton of ketchup now that Steven was doing the menu. Maybe if we didn't have to use so much ketchup we could afford better food.

When we were almost finished Steven said, just as casual as you please, "Maggie, did I tell you Mother's coming for a visit tomorrow? I'm picking her up in Chapel Hill in the morning." He said this like he was just reminding me of something he'd already told me.

Well, this went right through me. I was already worked up over everything else and now Steven had invited his mother to visit without even mentioning it to me. Steven knew Mother Presson and I never got along, which was why he was bringing it up now at the table. He figured I wouldn't make a scene at the table in front of everyone.

For the girl's sakes, I tried to be real calm. "Lord, Steven, she wasn't supposed to come 'til the girls' graduation in June. How long have you been planning this? You never even mentioned..."

"Well, she's coming and that's all there is to that." He took a last gulp of his coffee.

Well, my whole week had been decided and nobody even thought to mention it to me. Nobody thought I might have an opinion on the subject.

I was clearing the table when Steven locked himself in the den, Amy went to her room, and Jill went out to the garage workshop. A minute later, I heard the chain saw start.

While I was still washing dishes, Steven left the house for a while. He returned with six bags of groceries.

Special groceries that hadn't been on our menu in months.

He brushed past me, plopping the bags on the kitchen counter and said, "I think I'll shower and turn in early. I have that long trip to Chapel Hill in the morning."

"Steven, we need to talk," I said, pulling a can of Earl Grey tea from the sack. He buys generic tea for us, but his mother gets Earl Grey.

"There's nothing to talk about," he said. Then he went upstairs to shower like it was all settled.

When I heard the shower water running and Steven singing "Oklahoma" loud and off-key upstairs, I turned on the kitchen hot water full force till I heard him howl. With our old plumbing nothing but ice cold water was hitting him upstairs in the shower.

It was childish and nothing was solved but it made me feel a whole lot better.

Chapter Seven

Mother Presson visits us four times a year and stays exactly one week. One week is long enough to bring some culture into our lives. Long enough to do her duty and yet not so long our tacky ways rub off on her. If she stayed even one more day she'd see me beating my head against the walls, which would prove her point that *anyone* can live in Poplar Grove, which she loves to say over and over again.

For nineteen years Steven has told me, "You're being childish, Maggie Sweet. Being nice to Mother is a sign of maturity."

I've tried to be good. I mean, she *is* Steven's only living relative.

Used to, I got blinding headaches when she called me, "Steven's child-bride," 'cause I knew she meant Steven's little red-neck bride. I got bearing down pains when she'd say our house was "a doll-house" 'cause I knew she meant tiny and tacky. I'd all but foam at the mouth when she called Mother and Mama Dean "diamonds in the rough" 'cause I knew she really thought they were hicks. At night, after we were in bed, I'd cry to Steven, "Why should I have to be *that* mature?"

Saturday morning, while Steven drove to Chapel Hill, I bit my lip and did what I'd always done: cleaned the house, put the good percale sheets on the guest room bed, cooked two kinds of meat, five vegetables, crescent dinner rolls, a Dutch apple pie, a chocolate pie and a Dirt cake (the one with Oreos in it). Then, I made the girls set the dining room table with the works—the good tablecloth, cloth napkins, candles and flowers.

When Mother Presson visits, it's like the Almighty Himself is coming.

At two-thirty sharp, they pulled into the driveway and Steven all but carried his mother to the door on a pillow.

When I met them at the door, she brushed her cheek against mine, "Margaret, my dear, how are you?"

I choked back, "I'm doing all right," and said, "Very well, thank you." (She'd taught me to say it that way over the years.) When we went into the dining room, she took one look at the table I'd been so proud of and made a face like she had a migraine, moved the water glasses from left to right and whispered, "I don't think anyone else noticed, dear."

Steven looked like the children did when they had the colic.

The girls had been coached from the time they were babies so they knew the rules. Rule number one is, the first night of their grandmother's visit, they eat with us in the dining room and mind their manners. After that, it's every woman for herself.

We'd barely sat down at the table when Steven said, "Mother, it's such a shame that I'll be s-o-o b-u-s-y all week. I'll barely be here for meals. But, you and Maggie will have all the time in the world to visit."

While he said this, he sliced the ham and avoided everyone's eyes.

Everyone but Amy was nervous and shifty-eyed. 'Course, Amy and her grandmother have this special understanding, both of them being too good for the rest of us and all.

After dinner, Amy and her grandmother went out to the front room to have a *real* talk. Instead of having hurt feelings over not being included, Jill grinned and offered to help me with the dishes. She hummed as we worked, and I could see that far from feeling left out, she considered herself the twin with the naturally curly hair, her sister the twin with the Toni.

We were just finishing when the telephone rang. "Mama, it's Mama Dean," Jill sang, handing me the phone. Then she slipped out the back door to her chain saw and freedom.

Mother was working a swing shift at the hospital, so Mama Dean needed me to drive her to the doctor's Wednesday morning. Since Steven was already hiding in the den and Mother Presson was waiting to corner me in the front room, I stayed on the phone as long as possible, listening to all of Mama Dean's symptoms and all of her friend's symptoms, too.

We were just about to hang up when Mother Presson came into the kitchen. "Margaret, we really must talk," she hissed.

I figured it was serious. In nineteen years she'd never set foot in my kitchen before. I hung up the phone and followed her to the front room.

"Margaret, my dear, I'm on the horns of a dilemma. I wouldn't hurt your feelings for the world...I just feel it's worth it if I can salvage..." She sighed, then made a face like her teeth hurt. "Perhaps, I should just say it. After all, we *are* family. What I'm trying to say is...Amy is an exceptional child."

"Hmm," I said, wondering where in the world she

was going with this.

"You do want what's best for her, don't you?"

"Well...sure."

"Margaret...Amy is wasting herself here in Poplar Grove. Won't you please let her spend the summer with me in Chapel Hill?"

Oh, Lord. We'd just finished our first meal together and she was already starting. "Mother Presson, Amy is doing all right. She's in the school orchestra, the National Honor Society. Besides, Poplar Grove is her home."

Mother Presson closed her eyes and sighed. "I know, dear. And I could just weep for her."

I didn't say anything. I just sat there, wondering why Steven was never around when she started in like this. As far back as I could remember Steven has always been "s-o-o b-u-s-y" when his mother visited.

"I know you'll manage," he'd say on his way out the door to do good works for the church, the Sons of the Confederates, the Band Boosters. The last time she was here, I followed him out on the porch and shouted, "Steven Presson, charity begins at home." He acted like he hadn't heard me and drove off.

Monday morning, while I rushed around the kitchen fixing Mother Presson's breakfast, she was upstairs in bed, dressed in pink, lacy bed jacket and pearls, ringing a bell.

Now, I didn't mind serving her breakfast in bed. I didn't even mind the bed jacket and pearls. If she wanted to lay around all morning, dressed fit to kill, it was all right with me. But that bell was something else again. It's sterling. The kind people used to call their maids in the old days. When Mother Presson visited, I was the maid.

I couldn't help but notice that for such a delicate woman, her right arm (bell ringing arm) had the strength and endurance of a prize-fighter's. And to keep up her strength she'd ordered fresh-squeezed orange juice, a pot of Earl Grey tea, two 2-minute eggs, a huge slab of country ham and a toasted English muffin.

While I waited for the tea to brew and tried to ignore the bell, I wondered if there was such a thing as the perfect crime.

That's when the telephone rang.

"I'll be late tonight, don't wait dinner for me," Steven said.

"Steven, don't do this to me!"

"Are you there, Maggie? We must have a bad connection...I can't hear you...now, you girls have a nice visit," he said, just before he hung up.

I hung up wondering if Steven lived on Fantasy Island. Could he really think that since "girls" enjoy visiting and his mother and I are both "girls," we'd just naturally enjoy visiting with each other? But living on Fantasy Island was great for Steven. It freed him from the "what will I do with Mother?" problem, and he didn't have to feel guilty!

Mother Presson, who'd been quiet for about thirty seconds, picked that moment to ring the bell, and something in me snapped. I carried the tray up the stairs and while she was checking to see if I'd remembered everything, I swiped the bell and put it in my robe pocket.

When I got back to the kitchen, I hid the bell in the tea canister, poured myself a cup of coffee, and lit a cigarette, right there in the kitchen, in the middle of the morning.

For a long time, I sat there drinking coffee, smoking,

and wondering why in the world it had taken me so many years to think of hiding the bell.

Then, it hit me. I'd been raised to be a good woman.

When my daughters come to me for advice on their wedding day, the one thing I'll tell them is, never be a "good woman." Over the years, I've learned that good women get to carry their own groceries, take the children to the emergency room alone, help shingle the roof, and make due with appliances that haven't been right since 1976.

I'll tell my girls to be delicate. Steven's mother is delicate. She has enjoyed poor health since Steven's birth, forty-nine years ago. Delicate women get breakfast trays carried to them every day of their lives by good women. Delicate women get bad news broken to them gently, after the emergency has been handled, by guess who? Good women.

"Play the role," I'll tell my girls. "And play it to the hilt."

The day I told Steven I was expecting the twins, he got pale, made me sit down, waited on me hand and foot, and hated himself for being the no-account man who'd got me into that fix in the first place.

Did I bless his mother, who had paved the way for me to go back to bed with several good books 'til the babies were born? Lord, no. I was a good woman. I told him being pregnant was a normal condition, that I was strong and healthy and he shouldn't make a fuss.

He believed every word.

By the time I saw I wasn't as strong and healthy as I thought, Steven had decided that plenty of exercise was good for pregnant women. He never made a fuss again.

"But, Mama," my daughters might say, "How can you ask us to be so phony, so conniving, so unfair?"

And I'll say, "It's easy, sugars. It's real, real easy."

Tuesday afternoon, I took Mother Presson to Millie's Percolator Grill. They have the best steak sandwiches in town but she just picked at hers. After lunch we went shopping, which I hate, but I planned to keep her out of the house 'til Amy was home to entertain her.

My timing was perfect. Amy met us at the door. She could hardly wait to get her grandmother alone. They went to the front room so she could read an essay she'd written in English class: The Person I Admire Most—My Grandmother Presson.

While they read this little ditty over and over again, I did some things I enjoyed more, like hosing out the garbage cans and scrubbing the commode.

For two solid days, Steven and Jill stayed out of the house until dark.

After supper, Mama Dean called to remind me about her doctor appointment. She'd been busy, she said. Our town flasher had finally come to trial, so she'd been camped on the court house steps all week, hoping to get a peek at "Some filthy man getting his." I told her I wished I'd been with her and meant it.

At the clinic Wednesday morning, the receptionist told us that Dr. Helton, Mama Dean's regular female doctor, had been called away on an emergency. Dr. Pinckney, a male doctor, would be seeing all of Dr. Helton's patients. Mama Dean set her jaw, but went off with Patsy Jo, the nurse, when her name was called.

For the first time in days, I sat back and relaxed. It was wonderful. I flipped through the pages of *Mademoiselle* and thought about the reunion and Jerry. I wondered what I would wear now that my good beige church dress had gone all to pieces in the washer. Maybe I'd buy a new one—streak my hair, borrow Mary Price's sun-lamp. Maybe there was time to develop a bust.

Sinking into the Naugahyde couch, I thought back to high school when my future seemed filled with exciting possibilities. I was deep in thought when Patsy Jo came back to the waiting room. "Maggie, we need you in the examining room!"

While I'd been daydreaming about the reunion and Jerry, something had happened to Mama Dean! I was paying for my sinning in advance! I followed Patsy Jo's starched back up the hall, my mouth so dry I could barely whisper, "What's wrong?"

"Oh, Maggie, I'm sorry. I didn't mean to scare you. It's just...your grandmother won't let Dr. Pinckney near her."

When we got to the examining room, Mama Dean was sitting with her arms crossed over her chest, wearing her shoot-if-you-must-this-old-gray-head look.

Dr. Pinckney had dark hair and round glasses and reminded me of John Lennon. I liked him right away. I could see he was trying hard to stay patient with Mama Dean. Even though he smiled, he kept working his jaw muscles.

"Mrs. Presson, please tell your grandmother this examination is routine," he said.

"Mama Dean, this examination is routine," I repeated.

She just sat there. She didn't blink or budge. Finally, Patsy Jo took over, taking Mama Dean's blood pressure, weighing her, listening to her heart. When they were through, Dr. Pinckney said, "Mrs. Pruitt, have you had any problems since your last visit?"

Mama Dean glared at him like he'd insulted her, then she said, "You're the doctor. You tell me."

All the way home, she didn't say the first word. She just sat there in the passenger seat, her jaw pooched out, and her arms folded over her chest like an old Indian.

"Well, I hope you're proud of yourself," I said.

"Hmph."

"All you did was waste everyone's time."

"Hmph."

I wasn't getting anywhere. "All, right, Mama Dean, let's forget the whole thing. Next time we'll wait for Dr. Helton. I'm sure it won't hurt Dr. Pinckney's feelings one bit."

The traffic light in front of the bank turned red, so I stopped the car. On the next block, in front of Woolworth's, I saw a man who looked just like Jerry. I craned my neck. He had long, thin legs, the same shock of dark hair and the walk I thought I'd forgotten.

For years, I'd "seen" Jerry in malls, on the street, in every crowd. My heart would do flip-flops, but when I got closer it was always a tall, dark-haired stranger. It'd been years since I'd "seen" Jerry like that. I hoped all the reunion talk wouldn't start all those old feelings again.

By the time the light changed, the man had disappeared and Mama Dean was muttering something about, "Stinking man. Even with all those diplomas on the wall they all just want one thing."

I put the Jerry look-alike out of my mind and stepped on the gas. In a few minutes I'd drop off Mama Dean and go home. Then it hit me: why did I want to get home? Mother Presson was waiting for me at home!

Mama Dean sniffed and dabbed her eyes.

"Now what's wrong?" I said.

"Nothing. I'm fine! Just fine! Don't bother to take me home. I know you can't wait to get shed of me! Just drop me off here. You don't even have to slow the car. I'll jump!"

She was reading my mind! "That's not true, Mama Dean. You know it's not true. You're just being crabby."

"Hmph. And after all I've done for you..."

"Now, Mama Dean. I was just about to invite you home for lunch," I lied.

She looked at me. "Is that la-de-dah mother-in-law of yours still visiting?"

"Lord, yes. And she's driving me crazy. She's so picky if she makes it to heaven she'll demand to see the upstairs!"

"I accept."

"What?"

"I said, I accept. I will come to lunch."

Oh, Lord. I'd overplayed my hand. Mama Dean and Mother Presson in the same house! It'd be a disaster! They wouldn't have five words to say to each other. They didn't have the first thing in common.

But Mama Dean was actually humming—something that sounded like, "Ain't You Sorry Now You Rascal You."

It took them about five seconds to find something in common. That something was that they were both mad at *me*. It started with, "What that Maggie Sweet has done to me ever since the day she was born." Then it went on to all ungrateful children everywhere.

My friends and I had discussed ungrateful children hundreds of times, but I'd never served lunch while being talked about in my own house.

At first I tried to defend myself, Steven, my mother, and all ungrateful children, etc., etc., but they ignored me like the wallpaper on the wall.

When I couldn't take it anymore, I stomped upstairs and splashed cold water on my face 'til I was pretty sure I wouldn't have a stroke. Then I carried the hall phone into my bedroom and called Mary Price.

"This is Mary Price 'Got The Wedding Band Blues' Bumbalough. I can't come to the phone now but if you'll leave your name..."

Damn! The message-machine! I hung up, wondering if 'Wedding Band Blues' meant Mary Price had written a new song, or if she was fixing to leave Hoyt again.

When I finally went back downstairs, Mama Dean and Mother Presson were still at it, having a wonderful time lapping up the other's accounts of how "the children just don't understand."

Mother Presson had even invited Mama Dean to stay for supper, without asking me, which I didn't appreciate at all.

When Steven finally turned up, he got his feelings hurt because while they usually hung on his every word, tonight they were so busy talking they ignored him. He only looked confused when I whispered, "Some friendships are built on the bones of the enemy."

And loneliness too, I thought later, when Steven locked himself up in the den and didn't come out till I was in bed.

It rained again on Thursday. Around eleven, I was

staring out the kitchen window and fixing chicken salad for Mother Presson's lunch, when Steven slammed into the kitchen, drenched to the skin. He glared at me and said, "I've been sick all borning...then the car broke down on the way hombe so I had to walk a bile in the rain...oh, hell...I'm going to bed."

While he took a hot bath, I called Hootie's Garage, laid out whiskey, lemon, honey, cold tablets, aspirin, vitamin C and braced myself for the worst. Steven's a real booger when he's sick.

A few minutes later, I carried the thermometer and a hot toddy upstairs. Steven was sitting on the side of the bed with only a towel around him. When he snapped, "Does it take an act of Congress to get an aspirin around here? A man could die waiting for an aspirin!" I noticed he was getting a pot belly.

Just then, Mother Presson walked past the bedroom. Since I didn't want her to hear Steven picking on me, I stuck the thermometer in his mouth so he'd have to hush.

His temperature was 100.2 but I told him it was only 99. Anything over 99 is a sign to Steven he's fading fast, which makes him even crabbier.

"Are you just going to stand there? I'm freezing. Get me a blanket, the heating pad..."

I got the blanket, the heating pad, his terry cloth robe, fluffed his pillows and tried to ignore his tone of voice. When I couldn't ignore it anymore, I said, "Steven, I know you feel like pure crud, but it's just a cold. Now get some rest." Then I shut the bedroom door and went downstairs to finish Mother Presson's lunch.

After lunch, I washed two loads of laundry, carried a tray to Steven, tidied the kitchen, put the laundry away, made polite conversation with Mother Presson, carried another hot toddy upstairs, started supper, went back downstairs for the Vick's, the vaporizer, and vitamin C and carried them back upstairs.

At two o'clock, I remembered the girls. It was raining harder than ever and they'd be expecting to ride home with Steven. I threw on my slicker, waded out to my old second hand car, and prayed it would start.

They were just leaving the building when I pulled into the parking lot. Jill saw me and came running. Then I saw Amy, standing under a doorway, looking miserable. I didn't think she'd seen me, so I tapped the horn and waved. Her face went tight, then she looked around carefully and came running, too.

The radio played Helen Reddy's, "You and Me Against The World." I turned up the volume. When the girls were little, we'd played that song hundreds of times while we snuggled in the rocking chair, waiting for Steven to come home. I'd nuzzle their sweet, moist necks, while they giggled and begged, "One more time, Mommy. Let's sing it one more time."

I looked at my blonde, pretty daughters. They'd be graduating in a few weeks. This might be the last time I'd pick them up at school. My eyes misted. Lord, how I'd miss them. What would I do without them?

"Do you remember this song, girls?" There was a catch in my voice as I sang along with the radio. "You and me against the world, sometimes it seems it's you and me against the world..."

As I pulled into traffic, a truck passed, splashing water on the windshield. I turned the wipers on high, hit the defrost button, and went on singing, "and when one of us is gone, and some of us are left to carry on."

It wasn't 'til we passed the library that I noticed the

girls weren't singing; they weren't even speaking.

I stopped singing. "Sorry I was late.....Daddy got sick...his car broke down...and Grandmother Presson...well, I just got busy...time went by..." I rattled on, filling up the silence.

Amy sniffed.

"Amy, are you sick? I asked.

"I'm sick all right. Sick and tired." she snapped.

"Oh, shit, Amy! Don't start, " Jill said.

"Start what?" I asked, stupidly.

"Oh, just this car...the way you're dressed. Why can't you be like Mrs. Bloodworth?"

I looked at the car's worn upholstery, my faded jeans and T-shirt. While I was being mushy and sentimental, Amy wanted a mother who wore her hair in a chignon, clothes edged in silk ribbon and who spoke in a plantation accent. I was stung.

"Well excuse me, I didn't have time to get the diamond tiara out of the vault!" I snapped.

"Very funny," she said.

"God, Amy! Don't do us any favors! You don't have to ride with the peasants! You can always get out and walk," Jill said.

"What would be the point? I might as well ride now. Everyone's already seen us."

"You turd!" Jill hissed.

"Don't you curse at me! Mother, did you hear what she called me?"

My head pounded. The rain poured down. I couldn't see. I hit the wipers again, clicked off the radio. "Watch your language, Jill. And, Amy Elizabeth, if you say another word, I'll stop this car and you can walk."

"Yeah, right..." she sneered.

Just then, a car came hydroplaning toward us. I swerved, barely missing it. No one said another word.

By the time we got home, I was wet and shaking. But it wasn't over yet. Steven met us at the door, glared at me through bloodshot eyes and roared, "What kind of house is this? We're out of mouthwash."

"Steven, there's a monsoon out there! You'll have to gargle with salt water, at least until it stops," I said, peeling off my soaked slicker.

"Dammit, Maggie, I said I need mouthwash. Not one of your backwoods home remedies."

I was cold, wet, and tired. Steven stood over me, splotchy and red-faced with anger. The girls were fighting. A puddle was forming on the foyer rug. In the kitchen, a complicated half-cooked supper waited. After I cooked it, I'd make polite small-talk with Mother Presson, referee the girls, wash the dishes, clean the rug, and run up and down the stairs for Steven until bedtime. And while I was doing *everything*, they'd all be lounging around the house sneering that *I wasn't doing any of it right*.

Something in me snapped.

"You all must think I'm a magician! Well, I'm not! I'm a human being! I can't produce miracles! I can't even *produce* mouthwash! Why, if I was a magician, I swear I'd make you *all* disappear!"

Everyone looked shocked. Mother Presson coughed politely in the next room, but I didn't care. I didn't care when Steven stomped upstairs in a huff, or when Amy said, "Why do you have to pick on Daddy? Can' t you see he's sick?"

I didn't care when Jill, who'd been on my side, said, "Boy, you're in a rotten mood!"

I grabbed my slicker and slammed out the door.

The rain was coming down in sheets, now, but I didn't care. I drove to Eckerd's, bought a pack of Marlboros, lit one, then drove straight to Mary Price's. She wasn't home. I drove around town for awhile; I stopped at the Shirley's Curl & Swirl. The shop was closed. I had fifty cents in my pocket, the car was almost out of gas, but I wasn't going home.

A few minutes later, I passed the high school and considered becoming a filthy old bag lady who lived in a big cardboard box right next to the school building. Every morning, when a certain dignified biology teacher or a stuck-up high school senior went by, I'd follow them, shouting, "Don't you know me? It's Maggie Sweet. I'm just having a little drinky from a slightly used bottle. Wouldn't you all like one, too?" Then, I'd cackle, while everyone in town watched them duck into the school building.

I turned on the car radio. Elvis was singing, "I'm Caught In A Trap." Tears stung my eyes. I clicked off the radio, drove another block and pulled into the hospital parking lot.

Today, Mother was working second shift. Maybe it was her break time. We could have coffee. I'd calm down.

The hospital had been remodeled since the last time I'd been inside. Orange arrows led me from the lobby, down the corridor, past a fancy new gift shop, a waiting room filled with modern waiting-room furniture, plants and paintings. The arrows led to another long hall, then stopped at the cafeteria entrance.

The cafeteria was as dark and gloomy as ever. I was glad. It suited my mood. I got a cup of coffee, tossed two quarters into a Styrofoam cup near the register, and found a table in the darkest, gloomiest corner.

Suddenly, I was completely worn out. I lit another

cigarette, took a sip of the strong, black coffee. Why had I come here? Did I think I'd have a friendly chat with Mother and everything would be all right? Why, she'd take one look at me and know something was wrong. The last thing I wanted her to know was that I'd slammed out of my house and didn't want to go back.

The cafeteria lights flicked on, kitchen workers called to each other as they wiped tables, filled sugar and salt shakers, carried pans of food to the steam tables. In a few minutes everyone on second shift would be lining up for supper.

I stubbed out my cigarette, set my cup on a rack in the hall and followed a set of blue arrows to the rest room.

The rest room was new. There were mirrors that went up to the ceiling, then wrapped clear around the room.

When I tried to leave the rest room, the mirrors got me so turned around, I couldn't find the door. A woman came toward me. I stepped aside to let her pass. She stepped the same way and stood in front of me. I stepped to the right and she stepped the same way and blocked me again. Then she smiled a strained, nervous smile.

We tried it again. Side-step-block. Side-step-block. By the fourth time her cowering, nervous smile started to grate on me. She was one of those beaten-down, poor-me, hangdog types that made me want to shout, "Lord, woman, get a hold of yourself! Where's your back-bone? Stand up for yourself. Stop apologizing for being born!"

Finally, I spoke up. I figured if I didn't, we'd have spent all of eternity apologizing and side-stepping one another.

"Excuse me," I said.

And she said, "Excuse me," at the exact same time. That's when it hit me! I'd been side-stepping my own reflection! That cowering, simpering, nothing-of-a-woman, was me!

Friday night, the last night of Mother Presson's visit, we all sat down to supper together. Everyone's voices were careful and polite, but I wasn't really listening. My mind kept drifting back to the sad, tired woman in the hospital mirror.

We were finishing the beef stroganoff, when Steven (who hadn't been home all week) jerked me back to reality by saying, "I'm sorry you have to leave, Mother. Can't you stay with us another week?"

He looked confused when I kicked him under the table. It wasn't 'til Mother Presson said she was sorry but she had to leave that I took a deep breath and drifted off again.

The next morning, Jill and I fell all over each other carrying Mother Presson's belongings to the car. At the last minute, when she was already buckled in the passenger seat, I ran back to the kitchen and got the bell out of the tea canister. But, I waited 'til Steven actually turned the key in the ignition before I handed it to her.

The car motor sputtered and died.

Steven tried again. This time the engine roared into life, coughed like it had bronchitis and stopped dead. This time he smiled nervously and said, "I think the engine's flooded."

We all waited in the driveway for what seemed like hours. Finally, the car started.

As they backed down the driveway, Mother Presson

stuck her hand out the window and gave a Queen of England wave. It wasn't until Steven braked the car that I realized she was motioning to me.

When I got to the car, she smiled and patted my arm. "Now, Margaret, I'll be back in six weeks for the girls' graduation. Amy's future is at stake and we're running out of time."

A moment later they were gone.

The girls and I stood blinking in the driveway for a full minute. Back inside, I felt like a sponge that had been rung out once too often.

The girls went upstairs to shower. A while later, Amy, color-coordinated and neat as a pin, left the house to study with friends. Then, Jill, dressed like Pocahontas and carrying a duffel bag, left for the flea market with her long-haired friends.

I took two aspirins and went back to bed, but after tossing and turning for a half hour or so, gave up. I showered, scrubbed the tub, picked everyone's soggy towels off the bathroom floor, then, on impulse, I dropped my towel and stood naked in front of the full-length mirror.

Lordamercy! It was worse than I thought! My hair hung limp past my shoulders. There were circles as dark as bruises under my eyes. My legs were still good and the stretch marks on my breasts and stomach had faded to faint silvery lines, but when I turned sideways and sucked in my stomach, nothing moved. Also, my behind seemed lower than I remembered.

I wondered if Steven had noticed the changes in me. Then I remembered his pot belly. I'd never noticed his stomach at all until it was a full-fledged pot belly.

I stared for a while, wondering if pot bellies and stretch marks had as much to do with keeping couples

Styles by Maggie Sweet

faithful as church vows and children. It's easier to show a tired old body to a tired old husband than to risk yourself with someone new.

How did a new man feel about stretch marks put there by another man's children?

Was there time for plastic surgery before the reunion?

Did movie stars who went from affair to affair and marriage to marriage worry about such things?

Why was I even *thinking* about such things?

I got dressed and went out back to the glider to brood.

Ten minutes later, I was back in the bathroom with a copy of *Southern Hairdo* and the hair-cutting shears. I cut, moussed, and dried my hair into a style Mama Dean called "boiled and hung upside down to dry."

In the bedroom, I rummaged through the dresser drawers, found the snug jeans, purple T-shirt and big earrings Jill had given me for Christmas. I put them on, then painted up a little.

A few minutes later, I picked up the car keys and headed out the door.

Chapter Eight

All the way to Mary Price's, I grinned and patted my moussed curls. I felt sassy and reckless. I wanted to laugh out loud. For years Mary Price had shocked and surprised me. Now it was my turn.

Her Silverado was parked in the driveway, along with Hoyt's faded Econoline van and a pick-up with out-of-state license plates.

Through the screen, I could see Mary Price, Hoyt and another man having coffee at the kitchen table. I knocked on the door, then let myself in. Mary Price bolted from her chair when she saw me. "I tried to call you," she whispered, coming toward me.

I barely heard her. My eyes were glued to the man sitting at the table. He had dark hair, long, lanky legs and the bluest eyes in the world. It couldn't be! It wasn't possible! I hadn't laid eyes on him since high school. How on earth had he got here? It was the wrong time, the wrong place.

"Jerry?"

"Maggie Sweet, is that you?

"Lordhavemercy."

"Godamighty."

He stood, looked confused, then happy, then embarrassed.

"I was just passing. I'm in a hurry. I need to get

home..."

"Don't run off yet, Maggie. Have some coffee," Hoyt said, looking at Jerry and me, me and Jerry.

I gave up. We stood staring at each other. He was smiling. He took my hand. I wanted to fling my arms around him, wanted to say, I've been waiting for this moment all my life.

"It's good to see you, Maggie. You look great."

I touched my hair, thought about my morning makeover. Now, I was sweating. I probably looked awful. "Thanks. So do you."

I stared at him, couldn't take my eyes off him. He was more beautiful than I remembered. His hair was short and neat, just beginning to gray. There were crinkly lines around his eyes. Eyes that still had the power to dazzle me. I got lost in his eyes.

My legs were shaking. I sat down.

"I really did try to call you," Mary Price mumbled.

I thought about the note taped to the phone the night I'd stomped out of the house. I'd been too tired to call her back, too depressed by that sad woman in the mirror. But I should have known her call was important. Mary Price never called or came near me when Mother Presson visited.

There was a pause that seemed to last hours, but was probably only seconds.

"Well, well, if it isn't old home week," Hoyt said, too heartily.

I looked at Jerry's tanned arms: the hair that grew on them was spun gold. I looked at his hands. No wedding ring. I looked away.

"Jerry's come home," Mary Price said. "Got his retirement money from the Navy on Tuesday and by

Thursday he'd bought back his old family home place."

It *was* Jerry uptown the day of Mama Dean's doctor appointment! He'd been here this whole time.

"Yep. Put his money in his jeans and came on home. Right, old buddy?" Hoyt said.

Jerry grinned at me. "There's a lot to be said for home. After Brenda and I split, I figured I'd stay in Jacksonville to be near my son, Trey. But when he joined the Navy there didn't seem to be any reason to stick around. And I'd been thinking about home, must have thought about it a million times."

Oh, Lord, he was divorced and back in Poplar Grove for good!

He grinned at me. "I've been uptown a few times and I haven't seen it yet. Weren't you going to have a beauty shop...Styles by Maggie or something?"

I grinned back. He remembered. "Things changed. You were going to be a writer. Whatever happened to that?"

He laughed. "Lord, Maggie Sweet. You're the only one in the world who'd remember that, the only one who *knew* about it." He grinned at Mary Price and Hoyt. "Who would have thought it? All those years I tried to be this tough guy, but Maggie Sweet had my number all along. You all didn't know it, but I was really Dixie Burger's writer-in-residence."

Everyone laughed. Jerry reached over and filled my coffee mug. I stared at his arms, his long, slender fingers. Just talking about all our old dreams made me sick with longing.

I shook my head to clear it.

"Well, Maggie, we're fixing to ride out...see what all Jerry's got to do to the old place." Hoyt said.

"Everything needs doing," Jerry said. "But the Navy always called us Seabees the 'dirt Navy.' We built barracks, cleared land...only now it'll be *my* place, *my* land and I've got all the time in the world."

'All the time in the world.' He'd actually be *living* here. I'd be bumping into him everywhere! Suddenly, all the air went out of the room. If Jerry so much as looked at me again, I'd start hyperventilating, calling for a paper bag. I'd look like a fool, sitting here, in Mary Price's kitchen with a paper bag over my face!

I stood. "It was good to see you, Jerry. But, I've got to go...got a lot to do."

He stood. "It's been great seeing you. I wish you could stay. But I guess we'll be seeing each other all the time now."

Mary Price winked, "Thanks for the warning, right Maggie?"

This was where I was supposed to say something clever, some high school-line like, "Not if I see you first!" But nothing came to mind.

Thank heaven, Mary Price slipped her arm through mine and walked me to the door. Walking and breathing seemed to be a full-time job.

All the way home, my thoughts raced. What was I going to do? I'd never considered being unfaithful to Steven. Never even been tempted. Why had Jerry come here, now, at the most mixed-up, restless time in my life?

Then I remembered his eyes, the way the whole room seemed to disappear around him, just like the first time we'd met, all those years ago at the sock-hop. For years, I'd pushed Jerry's memory so far back in my mind that there were times I'd started to think that I'd made him up.

Made *us* up. Now, here he was. A live flesh and blood person; near at hand, just out of reach. It would be so easy.

You're not a love-struck teenager anymore. You're married! I know! You've got to stop this! I know! What are you gonna do? I don't know! You'll stay away! I'll stay away!

That night at supper, Steven said, "Well, for heaven's sake, Maggie. Aren't you going to comb your hair today?"

"It *is* combed. It's the latest style in *Southern Hairdo Magazine*.

"Then it's supposed to stick up like that," he said, trading a smirk with Amy.

My hands automatically smoothed my hair.

"Don't touch it, Mama. I like it!" Jill said.

"Thanks, Jill."

"Well, I wouldn't get too excited, Mama. We all know what tacky taste Jill has," Amy said.

I didn't say anything. I just looked at Amy.

"Now, Maggie, don't go getting your feelings hurt," Steven said. "All Amy's trying to say is you're thirty-eight, not eighteen. You've got to admit that middle-aged women look ridiculous when they try to look young."

That night, I dreamed I was in a woods, following a path through a heavy fog. The fog was so thick I could barely see, but I knew if I didn't stay on the path something awful would happen. I fumbled on, keeping my eyes down, concentrating on never letting my feet leave the path. At times the fog got so bad, I couldn't see the path at all. When that happened, I'd stand completely still, afraid that if I moved, even an inch, I'd get so far off the path, I'd never find my way back.

Then the fog would lift for a second and I'd take

another step or two before the path vanished again.

Suddenly, the path just stopped and I was at a cross-roads.

I stood there, staring at the Y in the road. There wasn't a single sign to guide me, to show me which road to take.

I looked back, toward the path I'd already taken, but it had vanished without a trace to show it had ever existed.

There was a sinking feeling in my stomach as I turned and faced the crossroads. I knew I had to decide which road to take, or stand in the same place for all of eternity.

Chapter Nine

Monday morning, after everyone left for school, I decided to stay too busy to think. I covered my hair with a bandanna and started the spring cleaning. I was defrosting the refrigerator when Mary Price knocked on the back door. She was dressed in a yellow cowgirl outfit, and carrying an Eckerd bag.

"Maggie Sweet," she said, pushing past me into the kitchen, "I've had the greatest idea in the world and you're the only one who can help me."

I froze. I hadn't talked to Mary Price since Saturday. For two days, I'd been hiding out in the house. I still wasn't ready to talk about Jerry, not even with Mary Price.

She went to the counter, poured herself a cup of coffee and lit a Virginia Slim, talking a blue streak the whole time.

"It's been a whole year since me and Hoyt started playing at the That'lldu. If I'da known we'd still be there I'da stuck my head in the oven and been done with it."

I relaxed. She wasn't here to talk about Jerry.

"It isn't that bad, Mary Price," I said, avoiding her eyes while I told this big lie.

"It is that bad," she said. "But something happened Saturday night that told me what I need to do to get out there."

"You're not going to quit, are you? I mean, it might

not be much, but the That'lldu is the only place that pays you cash money to sing."

"If you call that money! The way Hoyt manages us it's costing us money to work there. Anyway, I'm not quitting. Not yet."

She flopped down in a kitchen chair. "But what I've got in mind is my ticket out. I just know it'll start me and Hoyt on the road to fame and fortune."

She set the Eckerd bag on the table and pulled out a package of Lady Clairol Champagne Blonde hair color, plastic gloves and a beautician's cape.

"Well, Mary Price...what in the world?"

"That's what I'm trying to tell you! Saturday night, I was strutting my stuff, belting out a Tanya Tucker number..."

"I love Tanya."

"Me too. "Especially 'I'll Come Back As Another Woman,' which is something I'm fixin' to do."

"Lord, Mary Price!"

"I mean it. Saturday night, this old boy at the bar kept staring at me. Finally, during our break, he came over and said, 'Honey, you sound just like Tanya when you sing that song. You even look a little like her too.'" Then Mary Price started waving the boxes around, like I could read her mind.

"Saturday, when I saw your new hairstyle, I knew you could do it," she said, seeing she had to spell it out for me. "I want you to color my hair like this," she said, pulling out a record album with a picture of Tanya Tucker on the cover.

"You want me to bleach your hair?"

"Does Bubba drive a truck?" she asked. She tore the Clairol box open, like it was decided.

Stalling for time, I started a new pot of coffee. But Mary Price was already covering her cowgirl outfit with the cape.

"Mary Price, sometimes you worry me to death. You know this is a cut, rinse, set, kind of town. I haven't done a bleach job since beauty school. I mean, I get to do a precision cut now and then, or even a Frost 'N Tip, but never an out and out bleach job."

"Jumping Jesus, Maggie Sweet! You wouldn't recognize opportunity if it knocked you slam into next week. You've been talking about Style's By Maggie for years! Now I'm offering you the chance of a lifetime...a chance to be Maggie Sweet, hairdresser to the stars!"

"But, bleach, Mary Price! It could ruin you for life!"

"What's the worst that could happen?"

"Only that your hair could fall out! There isn't much call for Kojack lookalikes in the country-western field."

"Shoot! It's only hair. If it don't work out, it'll always grow back. Besides, I want you to whack most of it off anyway; one of those precision-cuts but not *too* precise. Sort of a cross between Tanya, Tammy, maybe a little Anne Murray. You know, my *own* look."

That's Mary Price all over. Impulsive and hard-headed. Once she gets an idea in her head, there's no talking to her. Also, I've noticed that since she's taken up country singing she talks country all the time. She doesn't have to. She just wants to. But she sure knew how to work me. Maggie Sweet, hairdresser to the stars, did have a nice ring to it.

After stalling all I could, I poured us both a cup of coffee, read the Lady Clairol directions over and over again, and then did it. I bleached her hair. 'Course the whole time I was slathering on the bleach goop, I kept praying that it would come out all right.

By lunch time we were finished and when I handed her the mirror, she was tickled to death. "Lord, Maggie Sweet, it's even better than I thought. I just hope Hoyt can stand all this beauty in one person!"

She was right. The short champagne blond hairdo suited her. All her life she'd had mousy brown hair. "Hair colored hair," she called it. 'Course her personality more than made up for it, but now her hair matched her personality.

When she got ready to leave, I followed her. It was like I couldn't stand to see her go. Because Mary Price had changed. She was all lit up, like someone had flipped on a switch. When she went out the back door, I had this terrible, sinking feeling that my old friend was gone forever, that this sparkling, shimmering stranger had taken her place.

I walked her out the driveway and as she got in the Silverado, I said, "Mary Price, what in the world is Hoyt going to say about all this?" (I didn't really care what Hoyt said, I was trying to keep her from leaving, from going out of my life.)

"I'll tell you what," she said, drilling me with her eyes. "All weekend, we fussed and argued. Finally this morning he said, 'Hell, Mary Price, why don't you just suit your own damned self. That's what you always do anyway.' Well, that flew all over me! I mean, if I'd been suiting myself I'da never been at the That'lldu in the first place. So I said, 'All right, Hoyt Bumbalough! I *will* suit myself.'"

She paused, then looked away. "I've been thinking how it's been twenty years since we left school. Twenty years, Maggie Sweet! And I've settled for being a second rate singer in a red-neck bar. Well, maybe I can't do any better than that, but I've got to try. I mean, even Toy Overcash was willing to try."

Until that moment, I'd always thought Mary Price was fearless. Now, I saw she was scared, just like me. Only, scared or not, she was going ahead anyway.

"Listen, Maggie Sweet, our lives are slipping by while we wait around for something to happen. Well, we can't just wait. There's no law that says a person has to settle. We've got talent, Maggie. We've got what it takes. We've just got to let everyone know it."

"Lord, Mary Price, I don't have any talent."

"You're only the best hair stylist in town. Only you've been so busy doing whatever it is housewives do that we all forgot. When I saw your new hairdo Saturday I thought, Lordymercy, I didn't know Maggie had it in her. I'm your best friend and even I didn't know. We've got to show them Maggie. And that's what I'm fixing to do."

Then she climbed into the truck, blew me a kiss, and drove off.

After she left, I stood on the porch for a long time. I wanted to chase the Silverado down the street, wanted to shout, "Mary Price, come back. Please don't leave me! I'm not ready. I need you to tell me what to do. I don't know what's right or wrong, what's brave or foolish."

And, then, because I didn't know what else to do, I dried my eyes and went back inside to finish the refrigerator.

Chapter Ten

That night, I drove to Winn-Dixie to pick up more Windex, Murphy's oil soap, and paste wax for the spring cleaning. It was the first time I'd left the house in days so I was kind of jumpy anyway. To make matters worse, I was barely through the door when I saw Dreama Nims pushing her grocery cart past the dog-food aisle.

Since Dreama was the last person I wanted to see, I ducked behind a paper towel display 'til she went on to the dairy lane.

When I saw her muu-muu disappear around the corner, I slipped up the cleaning-supply aisle, grabbed what I needed, and headed for the meat department to hide out 'til the coast was clear.

Darting to the back of the store, I saw a blond, spiked-haired woman in a yellow cowgirl suit, hug a tall, dark haired man near the T-bone steaks.

Lordhavemercy! It was Mary Price and Jerry! I froze. But Mary Price saw me and waved.

She came toward me. "I was just fixing to call you! Oh, Maggie, the most amazing thing in the world happened! You tell her, Jerry. I can't talk—I'm as jumpy as a cockroach in a hot skillet!"

Jerry smiled. "Should I start at the beginning or just blurt it out?"

"Well, Lord, Jerry, I could blurt it out! I want you

to start at the beginning, complete with the drum rolls!"

"All right. Here goes. It all started after Mary Price left your house this morning. She drove straight to Charlotte and found herself a talent agent..."

"Not just any talent agent," Mary Price interrupted. "The best talent agent in the entire Southeast! But, go ahead Jerry!"

Jerry laughed. "Well, the agent took one look at her yellow cowgirl suit and yellow hair and the poor woman was..."

"She was overcome! Completely overcome," Mary Price said, her eyes as big as soup tureens. "The next thing I knew she was listening to my tape, changing Hoyt's and my name to 'The Traveling Bumbaloughs' and by three o'clock we had a major audition!"

"An audition! Oh, Mary Price, that's wonderful!" I said.

"But it gets better! Oh, Maggie Sweet, we got the job! Saturday night we'll be one of the featured acts at Palomino Joe's!"

"I've heard about Palomino Joe's. They've got this big saw-dust covered floor for dancing, plank tables, pitchers of beer," Jerry filled in.

"And it's not just pickup bands, either. Vince and George and Charlie have all been through there and now *we're* the featured act! We've only got one set, but if they like us there's no telling. And I aim to see that they like us!" Mary Price said.

"You may touch her now," Jerry said. "'Course you'll have to get in line for autographs."

Mary Price took a deep stagy bow, then jumped up and spun around, "Oh, Maggie, I can't believe it! It's starting!"

Just then Hoyt came up the aisle carrying a bottle of champagne. When he saw us, he grinned, flung his arms around all of us, and hugged us tight.

"Oh, Lord!" I said, hanging onto them for dear life. They were my childhood, my history, my past—Mary Price and Hoyt, Maggie Sweet and Jerry, together 4-ever. I'd come home.

I started to cry.

Mary Price pulled away, "Lord, Maggie, don't. You'll have me bawling in a minute. We need to be dancing, not having a big old bawling session here in the Winn-Dixie."

"I guess I'm like your agent—completely overcome," I said, laughing through my tears.

Then Hoyt grabbed Mary Price and Jerry grabbed me and the four of us did a smooth combination line-dance, Texas-Two-Step, through the meat aisle.

Jerry held me tight. "Maggie Sweet, it's so good to be back! I wouldn't have missed this for anything in the world!"

That's when Dreama Nims nabbed us, laughing and dancing in the meat aisle at the Winn-Dixie.

Chapter Eleven

Dancing with Jerry at the Winn-Dixie had brought me back to life. But over the next few days I wondered if he'd saved my life or ruined it.

Tuesday morning, I lost my simple mind and drove past the city limits sign, the That'lldu, the JESUS OR HELL bridge, past the Dingler's house, the stand of loblolly pines, Belews Pond and wound up on Chatham Road.

Thank goodness, Jerry wasn't home. I don't know what would have happened if he'd been there. Would I have flung myself into his arms, lived out my schoolgirl dreams? Made a fool of myself? Wrecked everyone's lives?

It was such a close call that when I got back home, I was still shaking. Because while my heart was buckling at the knees, my head said, "For goodness sake, Maggie, you're thirty-eight, not eighteen. The time for dancing in the aisles is over."

While my heart said, "He's the one for you," my head said, "Your family's counting on you. You're a good Methodist girl from Poplar Grove, North Carolina. You can't change that. You can't go back on your raising."

But, spring cleaning, I'd catch myself line-dancing the oil-soap over the mahogany paneling, shagging the velvet drapes on down to the dry-cleaners, Western-swinging the steam-cleaner over the rugs and scrubbing the floors to George Strait's "Second Chance."

When Mary Price called, I was oil-soaping the

kitchen cupboards. "I've reserved a big table up front for my friends at Palomino Joe's Saturday night," she said.

This surprised me so, I didn't say anything.

"Maggie, are you still there? You are planning to go, aren't you?"

"Of course I'll be there. I wouldn't miss it for any-thing in the world," I said, not missing a beat. But, after we hung up, I realized I hadn't even thought about going to the opening. It wasn't that I didn't want to go. I was just so out of the habit of going anywhere, it never came to me to think that I *could* go. I'd never gone to see her at the That'lldu. Steven had had a hissy fit the one time I men-tioned it, so I dropped it. But Palomino Joe's was the biggest thing that had ever happened to Mary Price. I couldn't let her down again.

Later, it hit me, Jerry would probably be at Palomino Joe's, too. Just thinking about that made the spring cleaning go completely out of my head. I'd pick up the bottle of Windex and suddenly it was time to start sup-per. At night, I'd wake up thinking I was about to smother. Sometimes it got so bad, I'd have to get up and walk the floors. Other nights, I'd just lie awake for hours, listening to the strange pounding of my heart. Every heartbeat seemed to say, "This is *it*, Maggie Sweet, this is your life. This is *it*, Maggie Sweet, this is your *real* life.

Thursday, it came to me that with my feelings so stirred up over Jerry, I had to make Steven go to Palimino Joe's with me. I needed him glued to my side so no one could forget, even for a minute, that I had a husband—that I was a decent married woman.

That evening, the minute my courage was up, I barged into the den and blurted, "Steven, why can't we ever go out to someplace fun?"

He looked at me like my hair had turned green, and said what he always said, "You always want to do something we can't afford."

I started to remind him about the cemetery plots he'd bought, without a word to me, but I didn't have the energy. "You never once took me to see Hoyt and Mary Price at the That'lldu. Now they've had a big break. They're the featured act at Palomino Joe's Saturday and I want to go."

Steven snorted. "So that's it! You know I wouldn't set foot in a place like that. It's a waste of time and money. Besides, I don't even like country western music."

I started to say, I don't like historical meetings, tombstone rubbings, fund-raising banquets, or mahogany paneling. But I didn't say anything. I just stared at him.

He tried to go back to the papers he was grading, but when he saw I wasn't going anywhere, he sighed, took off his glasses and rubbed the bridge of his nose. "What's the matter with you? You're in the strangest mood lately. I heard you out there talking to yourself."

"I wasn't talking, I was singing. I use to sing all the time. Listen, Steven, Mary Price and Hoyt are my friends and Palomino Joe's is completely respectable."

Steven just rolled his eyes and sighed.

"If it was Theo Bloodworth asking, you'd go in a heartbeat," I rushed on. "Now it's *my* friends. I want to go. We could have fun. Lord, Steven, don't you ever want to do something fun? Does life always have to be the same old same old?"

"Life *is* the same old same old. I thought you knew that by now. We're not going and that's all there is to that. Next thing you'd want a new outfit; the expense would go on and on. Besides, I'm tired. I plan to rest on Saturday."

he said.

"But this is only Thursday. The opening's not 'til Saturday. How can you plan to be tired in *advance?*"

He put his glasses back on and rattled his papers. "I can't talk to you when you get like this. I *always* rest on Saturday. You know that. That's just how I am. Now if you don't mind, I've got work to do." Then he went back to his papers like everything was settled.

I stood there for a minute watching him, feeling all dead inside. Steven was only forty-nine years old, but he was the oldest man I knew.

When I got back to the kitchen, I thought, well, you just rest then, Steven. But just because you want to lay down and die doesn't mean I have to lay down next to you.

Then I picked up the phone.

"Mary Price, do I have to wear a cowgirl suit Saturday night or can I dress like a normal person?"

Chapter Twelve

Steven wasn't speaking to me. When he saw I was going to Palomino Joe's with or without him, he said, "I don't like the way you're acting. I've let you keep your friends, but I won't have you acting cheap." Then he went into the den and slammed the door.

After that he didn't say a word either to me or the girls. He stomped around the house in a huff, slamming doors, glaring at everyone. For two days, I cooked from the menu and tried to pretend everything was fine. Steven sat through our meals with his face and heart like stone, and the girls' eyes darted back and forth between us.

Saturday morning he left the house early without a word to anyone about where he was going or when he'd be back.

The silence shouldn't have bothered me. I should have been an expert at Steven not speaking. But the tension in the house had my nerves torn to pieces.

Saturday, I almost called Mary Price a dozen times to cancel.

All morning, I brooded around the house. But that afternoon, I went upstairs and dippity-dood my hair straight up for courage. I was in the bathroom, staring into the mirror, when Amy strolled in. She didn't seem to notice me. She picked up a hairbrush and started flipping the ends of her pageboy. Then all at once her eyes went wide.

"For heaven's sake, Mama! It's bad enough to have a sister who thinks she's Sacajawea. Now, my own mother thinks she's Tina Turner."

"Do you think this hairdo's all right for Palomino Joe's tonight?"

She stared at me. "You, going to Palomino Joe's? What for?"

"To watch Mary Price and Hoyt perform."

"Honestly, Mother! Only rednecks and redneck wannabes go the Palomino."

"You sound like a big old snob when you talk like that, Amy"

She sniffed. "I can't believe you talked Daddy into taking you."

"Daddy's not going."

"You mean you're going without him?"

"Daddy doesn't want to go. But Mary Price and Hoyt are the featured act. I think I should be there."

"I can't believe it! I think it's bizarre! Mrs. Bumbalough strutting around town in a cowgirl suit and now you! Why, it's positively bizarre! Why can't you be like other mothers? What if someone sees you?"

"Everyone will see me! The whole town's going, including mothers! Now, watch how you talk to me. I'm still your mother!"

"A mother who goes to bars! Dances with rednecks! I can't believe you'd do anything that low!" She threw the hairbrush into the sink and ran out of the bathroom and down the stairs.

I ran after her. I wanted to pinch her head off. "Amy, come back here! I'm not through with you!"

She didn't slow down, just looked over her shoulder

and shouted, "I'm the one that's through! I can't stand it! The minute I graduate I'm moving in with Grandmother Presson!"

After she left, I went upstairs and threw myself on my bed. I'd been so excited about feeling alive again. But the minute I was singing around the house, looking forward to something, Steven stopped speaking to me and Amy started threatening to leave home.

From the bed, I could see my reflection in the dresser mirror. My hair was sticking straight up. A few minutes ago it'd given me courage. Now I felt like a fool. Maybe Steven and Amy were right. Maybe I was a silly middle aged woman trying to look young. I frowned at my reflection, mashed my hair flat. Me, going to Palomino Joe's, what for? Was it really to see the Bumbaloughs or just an excuse to see Jerry again? Maybe I was a thirty-eight year old woman looking for romance and excitement, when the time for romance and excitement were over.

I went downstairs and picked up the phone to call Mary Price, but no one answered.

Ten minutes later she knocked on the door.

"I know I'm hours early, but I'm too wound up to wait. Can you do my hair now?"

We went to the kitchen and I poured two cups of coffee. "I was just about to call you. Would you...be mad... if I didn't go tonight?"

She just looked at me. "Well, Lord, Maggie. I can't believe it! I thought you wanted to go. You've said so all week."

I had hurt her feelings, the last thing I'd wanted to do. "Mary Price, I'm sorry. I want to go. I do. It's just...Steven's in a snit; he hasn't spoken to me in days. Then, this morning, Amy had a fit and ran out of the house."

"Is that all?" she said, lighting a Virginia Slim.

"Isn't that enough?"

"So Steven's mad. So what? Hoyt's mad at me half the time and the sun still comes up in the morning. Besides, teenagers are supposed to pitch fits. That's their job. 'Course I have to admit Amy's *extra* good at her job. But you can't let them get away with it."

"It's just...I hate when people get mad at me."

"Lord, Maggie. You've spent your whole life letting everyone tell you what to do. No offense, honey, but you even let your daddy tell you how to live your life and the Lord and everyone else knows that Smiling Jack Sweet doesn't have the sense God gave a goose."

Before I could defend Daddy she went on. "'Course you were only a child then, so I'll make some allowances. But you're grown now. Why, before I'd let my husband or child or anyone tell me what to do I'd dye my hair green and go braless to the Winn-Dixie. Just ask Hoyt Bumbalough if I wouldn't. I mean, what's Amy going to do about it? What's Steven going to do? Hit you? Chain you up in the basement? Thousands of women go out without their husbands every night of the week."

"It's not like that. Steven's a good man. He'd never hit me. It's just when he goes around not speaking, it makes me feel like pure crud."

She ground out her cigarette, then looked me in the eye. "If he's such a good man he wouldn't make you feel like crud over nothing. Just because he's not a criminal doesn't make him a good man."

"Well, for goodness sake, Mary Price," I gasped. Her logic always surprised me, spun my head around. I'd always placed Steven above me. He was the grown-up, I was the child. He gave the orders; I obeyed. But Mary Price wasn't the least impressed with Steven. She just saw him as another spoiled, bossy man. Why, if I'd said much more, she'd have met him at the door with a hickory switch.

"There's more to life than keeping your head down and cooking from the menu in hopes your husband'll do you the honor of speaking to you. He's just pouting like a spoiled child. He's had his way so long he thinks it's his due. But, this is America, Maggie. Lincoln freed the slaves. Tell Steven the next time he's at one of his historical meetings to look that up in his Emancipation Proclamation!"

I laughed. Already I felt better. Then, I thought about Jerry.

"Mary Price, I'm so mixed up. I just...I'm scared to death to see Jerry again," I said, avoiding her eyes.

She hesitated. "I wondered about that. I saw the way you two looked at each other the other day."

"You *saw* it?"

"Shoot! Even Hoyt saw it. And he doesn't notice anything. After you all left, he said, 'Mary Price, I'd die a happy man if you ever once looked at me like Maggie looked at Jerry. Why, she was lit up like Christmas.'"

"Oh, Lord, I'm doomed! What am I gonna do?" I wailed.

"You gotta do what you gotta do. But if it helps at all, Jerry won't be there tonight. His house in Jacksonville sold and he had to make a last minute trip down to Florida for the closing. Go tonight. Get your mind off your worries one night. But I'll tell you what, if a man ever looked at me like Jerry Roberts looks at you, I'd go to hell and face the devil before I walked away from it."

We sat there awhile, not saying anything. Finally,

Mary Price sighed and said, "Now, let's do my hair, then we'll figure out what you're gonna wear to the opening."

After finishing her hair, we went upstairs and looked in my closet. She took one look and said, "Jumping Jesus, it looks like Minnie Pearl's closet."

"Not everyone thinks cowgirl outfits are the height of fashion," I said.

"Sad but true," she said shaking her head. "Wear the jeans you wore to my house. They fit great. With boots and a scarf you'll be fine."

"But, I don't have boots," I said.

"You're kidding! What do you have?" she asked.

"K-Mart sneakers and my good beige pumps."

"Lordymercy, that's pitiful. Try these." she said, kicking off her own boots.

Five minutes later, I was dressed in jeans, a bright T and Mary Price's boots.

Just then, Jill, who'd come home while I was doing Mary Price's hair, peeked in the door. "What are you all doing? I could hear you laughing all the way downstairs."

"I'm doing a makeover on your mama. She's going to the Palomino tonight and she's gotta look good."

"MAMA! GOING TO THE PALOMINO!"

"If you've come to yell at me you'll have to get in line!" I snapped.

"Kick butt."

"What?"

"Kick butt! I wondered when you'd get a bellyful of the dead-relatives routine."

Mary Price gave me her "I-told-you-you-just-had-to-stand-up-to-them" look.

I wanted to say, Jill's easy. But you couldn't convince Steven and Amy in a lifetime.

Ten minutes later, I'd painted up, redone my hair, and Jill had loaned me an Indian print vest and turquoise earrings.

Mary Price dragged me to the mirror. "Lord, girl. I'll have to say you clean up good! I think we're ready for Palomino Joe's. I just wonder if Palomino Joe's is ready for us!"

I smiled at my reflection. An hour earlier I'd felt lower than a well. Now I felt great. "Thanks," I said, turning around to admire my new look. "But it should've been me helping you get ready for *your* big night."

"But, I *am* ready, Maggie. I've been ready for years."

"And now I'm ready, too," I said with feeling. "But, I want you to promise me something. If you all see me wallowing in nerves and self-pity again, promise you'll shoot me—put me out of my misery."

"You know I'd do anything for you, Maggie," Mary Price said, grinning at me in the mirror.

Chapter Thirteen

Palomino Joe's is a big, square, windowless building filled with picnic-style tables, a bar at one end, a bandstand at the other, and a huge sawdust covered dance floor in between.

Saturday night, two hundred people of every age, shape and size (everyone but Jerry) crowded the floor while The Traveling Bumbaloughs sang the oldies, "You Picked A Fine Time To Leave Me, Lucille," "Delta Dawn," "Satin Sheets," then the newer, "Modern Day Romance" and "She's Single Again." Toward the end of the first set, Mary Price winked right at me and sang, "Walking After Midnight."

I have to admit, I shed a few tears. I had always known what singing meant to Mary Price. Now I was choked with pride. She strutted all over the stage while her voice filled the room, owned the room and everyone in it.

I couldn't sit still. It was all I could do not to throw my head back and howl. I tapped my feet, drummed the table top, wanted to shout, "That's my friend! That's my best friend!" like a Little League parent whose child just hit a home run.

A whole new world was opening up to me. While I'd spent Saturday nights at committee meetings, or at home watching Steven rest, then having routine right-after-the-11:00-news-sex, some of Poplar Grove's finest were stomping it up at places like Palomino Joe's.

Geneva and Modine volunteered their husbands to dance with me, and I line-danced with everyone. But I was happy just sipping Pepsi, listening to the music and watching everyone.

Around ten, the Bumbaloughs took a break, and the pick-up bands were thrilled for a chance to make music.

Mary Price dragged me off to her dressing room to re-do her hair. "Hot-damn, Maggie! This is the night I was put on earth for!"

"I never knew you were this good!" I said, hugging her.

"I've never *been* this good! It's like something's come over me. Hurry with my hair. They've asked us to do another set and I don't want them to see that the pick-up bands are good, too."

When she went back to the bandstand, I looked at my watch. If I didn't get home soon, Steven would never let me out of the house again. But suddenly the energy level in the room went into high-gear. A spotlight hit Mary Price and everyone started to whistle and stomp. Even a tourist like me knew something special was happening.

She took stage-center and shouted, "Are you all having a good time?"

The crowd screamed, "YES!"

"Are you ready for a song about a low-down woman going low-down places!"

They shouted back, "We're ready!"

"I can't hear you!" she called.

"WE'RE READY!"

The music started, then built—Mary Price at the keyboard, Hoyt at the microphone. Whole tables of people circled the floor, grabbing the belt-loops of the person in front of them while they sang-shouted, "Ruby, Don't Take Your Love To Town," to the rowdy Bumbalough beat.

Modine and Ellis dragged me to the floor, and off we went, joining the line, dancing our feet off 'til we collapsed back at the table.

As soon as I stopped panting, I picked up my purse and started to say my goodbyes. That's when he came up behind me.

"Looks like I got here in the nick of time. How 'bout the last dance?"

I knew who it was without looking. I stood, put my arms around him and we moved to the dance floor. Mary Price was singing "You Were Always On My Mind." We didn't miss a beat.

Nothing had changed in twenty years. He was still a mile taller. It still didn't matter. I laid my head on his chest. Good Lord.

"We haven't had a chance to talk since I got back." he said.

"I know."

"Why didn't we run off graduation day?"

"I called you."

"When?"

"Graduation day."

He stepped back, looked in my eyes. "You did? I forget. I was crazy back then. Crazy from wanting you."

"You weren't home. I didn't know what to do."

"God. All those years," he said, pulling me close. "All those years...."

"I didn't know you still wanted..."

"I know."

"Godamighty."

"Oh, Lord."

We went back to our table. Two hundred sets of eyes watched us. He didn't say, I'll call. I didn't say, we shouldn't. We just knew.

Chapter Fourteen

Monday morning, I drove out to his old homeplace. I don't remember the drive; it was like a dream. But, I couldn't *not* go anymore than I couldn't not breathe. I didn't think about the cost or how long it would last. It didn't matter. Deep down inside, I knew it was my last chance forever.

I hadn't told him I was coming, but he met me in the yard.

He just looked at me; nobody had ever looked at me like that before. Then he took my hand and we went inside.

There are no words. Music comes the closest thing to what it was like to make love after all those years. But to say that making love with Jerry was like "Unchained Melody" or "The First Time I Ever Saw Your Face," isn't enough. To say there were times when I didn't know where he left off and I began, that I was him and he was me, comes close.

Afterward, he held me. "Where've we been all these years?"

"I don't know."

"I remember we broke up. You moved away..."

"Daddy came for me graduation day. He'd signed me up for school in Chapel Hill. I had to go. I had an hour to get ready; that's when I called you."

"I didn't know. I didn't get your letter 'til September. By then it was too late. I was in too deep," he said.

I'd forgotten about the letter I'd written from Daddy's that summer—a letter full of longing and empty pride.

"Someone forwarded it to me in Jacksonville but it was weeks before it caught up with me," he went on. "All that summer, all I could think about was getting over you. I bought a motorcycle, did some drinking, the whole James Dean bit. You always saw through my hood act, but Brenda believed it. Next thing I knew she was pregnant; we were married. I thought it was the right thing to do. But how could it be right when we didn't even know each other?"

"You raised your son," I said.

"Yeah. Trey was the one good thing that came out of it. But I stayed too long...like I had this spare life to throw away. I thought I could squander all those years and still have this other life waiting for me." He shook his head as if to clear it. "Can you understand? Does that make any sense?"

I remembered back to when I met Steven. My heart was broken. He said he loved me. I thought it was enough. I thought he was grown up enough for both of us, that he knew the ways of the world. We married and nine months later the girls were born. And even after I knew I'd married a stranger, I still believed if I was good enough, tried hard enough, stayed with it long enough, sooner or later it would be enough.

"You kept waiting around for your real life to begin," I said.

He propped himself on his elbow, gazed at me. "You know, don't you?"

I nodded, reached for his hand. He'd said more in an hour than Steven had said in nineteen years. He looked me in the eye, let me finish my sentences, heard what I said, what I *meant*. After all our years together, Steven and I still didn't know how each other's minds worked. But Jerry and I were on the same wavelength.

We lay there, holding onto each other, neither of us saying anything. Finally, I said, "Do you think two seventeen year old kids could have been in love for real? That maybe they *were* each other's real life?"

"I know I loved you to pieces."

"And I thought you'd hung the moon."

I held onto him. It *had* been real. Over the years I'd started to wonder if I'd made it up. But we really had loved each other.

Later, after we drank coffee, he took me on a tour of the house. It was smaller, gloomier than I remembered. "It's dark as a cave in here, but I plan to change that. I want light, lots of light," he said. "I might not even hang curtains."

I noticed paint cans stacked neatly in the corner. Cream and gold paint. The colors I'd wanted for *my* house. The same wavelength.

When it was time to go, Jerry walked me to my car, "I won't call you, Maggie. Today might just have been one of those things, something we needed to do to put 'The End' to Maggie and Jerry."

"Jerry, don't..."

He brushed my lips with his finger. "Hush. I mean it. I want you to think about it. My divorce will be final in June. It's you that'll be in a mess. You're the one with everything to lose. If we don't see each other like this again, just know that I loved you then, I love you now, I'll always love you. Maybe that's enough."

I touched his cheek. I'd come here out of awful longing. He'd given me back a part of myself that had been missing—I was him and he was me. It didn't matter what anybody said or how messy it would get. I had to have him. I loved him blood and bone.

Chapter Fifteen

"Are you alone?"

"You said you wouldn't call."

"I know."

"It's all right. I'm alone."

"I know. I drove by your house. The LTD was gone; only your old car was there."

"I miss you like crazy."

"No second thoughts?"

"Sure. Second and third thoughts. And they all make me run slam out of breath."

"When can you get here?"

"I'm leaving right now."

"Good. I've got a surprise for you."

When I got there, he said, "Close your eyes."

I closed my eyes and stood there while he turned on music and took me in his arms, waltzed me through the farmhouse to "A Rose And A Baby Ruth."

"Do you remember?"

"Our old song."

"I found it unpacking some boxes. Lord, Maggie, there were so many memories. I spent last night going through old photos, the prom, picnics at the pond...remember our first Christmas?"

Like so many of my Jerry-memories, I'd shoved that

first Christmas so far back in my mind it seemed to have happened to another girl, another life. But now that Jerry was here, it was safe to remember.

I held him close, followed his steps and thought back to the Christmas Eve we'd parked on a hillside on the outskirts of town. We got so lost in necking, we didn't notice how much time had passed. Suddenly, the whole world lit up like daylight. We both panicked, thinking it *was* daylight. But, it had snowed. The windshield sparkled like diamonds and there was an unearthly stillness as pure white silent snow drifted down. We'd never seen a white Christmas in Poplar Grove. It seemed like a miracle. We sat there holding onto each other, as hushed as in church. I remember thinking, you will never in your life be as happy as you are at this moment.

Tears stung my eyes. "It was like we were the only two people on earth."

"Like we were meant to see it together," he said, as he led me to the couch to Emmy Lou Harris' "Together Again."

I went back to Chatham Road three times that first week. And when I couldn't be there, I was planning to be there. It was just like the old days. I'd have walked through fire to be with Jerry.

But I didn't have to. Steven stayed locked in his den and the girls were busy with their own lives. I went through the motions, cleaned the house, did laundry and cooked from the menu; looked and acted, for the world, like the old Maggie Sweet. But I was someone else now. There was music in my head all the time and I couldn't stop smiling. It shocked me that nobody else saw it. I figured the change in me stuck out like new paint. Everything seemed different, clearer; scents were sharper, colors brighter. I felt new again. I wanted to run out in the yard and turn cartwheels.

Apart from being in love, other things were changing, too. Two women who'd been at the Bumbaloughs opening called me to do their hair.

Early one morning, after dropping off a dozen brownies for the Band Booster's bake sale, I stopped by the Zippy Mart and bought two Styrofoam cups of coffee and four muffins. Then, on impulse, I went to a pay phone and invited myself to the farmhouse.

When I got there, Jerry was sitting on the back porch steps.

We sat side by side, sharing the coffee and muffins, breathing in the scents of the early morning air. After we finished, he said, "I want to show you something."

He took my hand and led me to one of the out buildings. "This was my dad's machine shop when this place was a working farm. I've been clearing it out. I'm thinking about starting a carpentry business—you know, building kitchen cabinets, custom furniture for people. With my Navy pension and benefits I don't have to make a lot of money. Brenda always planned for me to take over her father's insurance business, but that wasn't for me. I've always liked working with wood. What do you think, Maggie?

"This building will be perfect."

"What do you think about me doing carpentry work? I'll never get rich. But it's satisfying work."

"Money isn't everything. Not if you've got enough to get by. I want you to do what you want to do. If you're happy, I'm happy."

Jerry grinned and spent the next twenty minutes showing me how he planned to set up his shop.

Later, when we stepped out into the sunshine, he said, "Do you feel like walking? There's something else I've been dying to show you."

He took my hand as we walked past the out buildings, across a field of freshly mowed grass, then climbed a split rail fence at the property line. The sun shone through the tree tops, making them look like green lace against the sky.

I heard the creek before I saw it, a few feet into the woods.

"I walked down here the other night. I remembered that the creek ran the length of Chatham Road. But it's closer to the house than I remembered. I wish you could have seen it with me at sunset. All those colors..."

We kicked off our shoes, rolled up our pant legs, and sat on a log, dangling our feet in the water.

I leaned back into his arms and told him about my two new hair customers.

"You never said. Why did you give up doing hair in the first place?"

I looked off into the distance. "That's a long story."

"I've got all day."

I took a deep breath. "When Steven and I first got married, he told me to wait. He was older—sure of himself. I wasn't sure about anything. I figured he knew best, that he'd given it a lot of thought and had our best interest at heart. I waited when the girls started school, then on through high school. Last year, when they started their senior year, I asked him again. He wouldn't even talk about it, just stomped off in a huff. That's when I knew it was never going to happen, that Steven never meant for me to work. I'd trusted him—believed that if I did the right thing everything would turn out all right. But all he'd really wanted for us was to live our lives *his* way. I felt like a fool."

Jerry held me close. I could feel his breath on my neck. "Why did *you* feel like a fool?"

"All those years I'd been kidding myself. I should have known that he'd never let me be a beautician."

"But you were in beauty school when you started seeing him."

"Yeah. But then I was only Maggie Sweet. It was all right for Maggie Sweet to be a beautician. It wasn't all right for Mrs. Steven Presson. Everyone seemed to think I was lucky to have him, that I had this great life. Finally, I gave up. I told myself it didn't matter, that I'd just be whatever it was everyone wanted me to be."

He turned my face toward his. "Steven's the fool—he doesn't know what you're worth. If your work makes you happy, he should want it for you. Lord, honey, I feel like you do. If you're happy, I'm happy. It's as simple as that."

I looked into his eyes. For us, it was as simple as that.

Chapter Sixteen

Naturally, feeling that happy couldn't go on forever, not for a good Methodist girl from Poplar Grove, North Carolina.

It started with Mama Dean calling to let me know she wasn't speaking to me. She does this by phoning but not saying anything. She just breathes into the receiver.

The first time she did this, I thought it was an obscene caller. Now, she's done it so often I recognize her breathing.

"Mama Dean, is that you?"

Silence.

"Mama Dean, I know it's you. I can hear you breathing."

More silence.

"Mama Dean, whatever it is, I apologize. Just tell me what I did or didn't do."

Dead silence.

By now I was wishing it *was* an obscene caller. An obscene caller would be a lot easier to deal with than Mama Dean. At least I could slam the receiver or blow a whistle into the phone on one of them.

"Mama Dean, if you don't say something in five seconds I'll figure it's a pervert and hang up."

She gasped at the word pervert, then her breathing went back to normal.

I hung up, then redialed. The line was busy. I hung up again, redialed again. This time the phone rang and rang. Finally, someone answered.

"Mother?"

"What in the world's going on? I had to get out of the shower to answer the phone. Here's me dripping all over the carpet and Mama's sitting there glaring at the phone but letting it ring away."

"She called me up not speaking," I said.

"Oh, Lord, Maggie. What have you gone and done?" Mother asked.

"That's the thing; I don't know."

"All right, I'll find out and call you back."

Two minutes later the phone rang. "She says she's not talking to you 'cause you were supposed to come and do her hair this morning."

"Oh, Lord, Mother, I forgot."

"She says she had to go uptown with her head in a polka-dotted roller-bonnet. She says she looked like a haint and it's all your fault."

"Tell her I'm sorry. Tell her I'll be out first thing in the morning. I'll even throw in a manicure," I said.

"She says you needn't to bother. She says because of you, everyone thinks she's the town character."

"But she is the town character!"

"Maggie Sweet, that's not the least bit funny. Do you really want me to tell her that?"

"No, Mother. She's just got me worn out. Tell me what to do. I'll do anything you say."

"I think you better come tomorrow and plan to stay and stay."

"You mean pay and pay," I said, feeling depressed.

"Well, Maggie Sweet, what a thing to say!"

"I know, Mother. But, sometimes I think I've been paying my whole life."

It was dark when I drove to the pay phone in Dixie Burger's parking lot. Inside, someone was playing Patsy Cline's, "Crazy."

"I can't see you in the morning. I was supposed to do Mama Dean's hair this morning but someone....uh.... side-tracked me and I forgot. Now she's mad."

"There's a lot of that 'sidetracking' going around. This morning, a pretty brown-haired woman sidetracked me for hours. Made me forget everything."

"I miss you already."

"Honey, I need to ask you, does your Mama Dean still follow you around?"

I thought back to high school when Mama Dean really did follow me.

"No. She doesn't get around like she once did. But she's still someone to reckon with. She called me up today, not speaking."

"What?"

"She calls on the phone but won't speak, just breathes. When your grandmother calls you up and breathes into the phone it'll make you feel guilty as home-made sin."

"Guilty about us?"

"Never about us; just about forgetting Mama Dean. I wouldn't hurt her feelings for the world. And I have to be careful. If she gets suspicious we're doomed. She'd call out her bloodhounds in a heartbeat."

"That paints a picture."

"I know. I'll see you after lunch. Don't cook."

The next morning, along with the manicure set and

hairdo supplies, I carried chicken salad and an Impossible Pie to the boarding house.

Mother, who was working second shift at the hospital, met me at the door. She was dressed in a pink housecoat and smelled like Jergen's lotion as usual. When she hugged me, she whispered, "Mama Dean's on the warpath. Look out."

I pasted a smile on my face and called out, "Hey, Mama Dean! I brought your favorites for lunch."

Mama Dean was sitting in her rocking chair, wearing the polka-dotted roller-bonnet over wet shampooed hair and an inside-out housecoat held together with three big safety pins. "Well, look what the cat's done drug in," she said.

I put the chicken salad in the refrigerator, cut three slices of pie, poured coffee, and carried everything on a tray to the front room. "Have you all been doing all right?" I was determined not to let her get me down.

"You're the one whose been so almighty busy," Mama Dean said.

"I *have* been busy," I said, avoiding her eyes.

"I see you had enough time to do your hair different. It looks like it's been boiled and hung upside down to dry," she sniffed.

I patted my hair nervously. Had it really been that long? I'd done my hair weeks ago. Then, I remembered: I'd done Mama Dean's hair last week and the week before that. I'd only missed yesterday because it wasn't our regular day. Mama Dean was setting me up, spoiling for a fight. But I didn't have to take the bait.

"Now, Mama Dean, you know I was here last week. You said you loved my hairdo. Why, I was planning to try it on you today," I said, winking at Mother.

"Well, sister, who put Tabasco sauce in *your* oatmeal?" she snapped. "I never said any such. I don't hold with that newfangled bull; old fashioned hairdos, old fashioned morals. Why, the hairdos and the morals in this town is already going downhill in a handbasket."

"Now, Mama, hairdos don't have a thing to do with morals," Mother said. "Remember how worked up you got when crew cuts came into style? You said all the boys looked like death row convicts and most of 'em grew up just fine."

"But now it's the women looking like convicts. I never thought I'd live to see any such. I saw Mary Price uptown the other day in a crew cut as yellow as a pumpkin. I swanee, she looked wild as a buck."

"Now, Mama Dean, you know Mary Price is in show business. She's supposed to look different than real life," I said.

"Hmph. Show business or monkey-business, she looks wild as a buck. You always did admire wildness, though. You take after your daddy that way."

I smiled helplessly at Mother, unpacked my comb, a round brush, rollers, setting gel and hair spray. "I did Mary Price's hair for her opening at Palomino Joe's," I said.

"Hmph. I wouldn't brag on it."

I dropped the subject of Mary Price and Palomino Joe's and started combing Mama Dean's hair. Mother's radio was playing "Tennessee Waltz."

Mama Dean said, "I think you young people are losing your simple minds. I heard about Toy Overcash. She ought to count her blessings. A good husband and all those children. Then she runs off over a' art studio."

"Who told you about that?"

"Mama ran into Dreama Nims uptown the other

day," Mother said.

"Why do you listen to that old gossip?" I asked.

"Well, I don't get around like I once did and no one around here tells me a thing," Mama Dean said.

"That's because it's over and it didn't amount to a hill of beans. I just hate and despise Dreama Nims. She's a gossip and a liar," I said.

"Well, sister, what a thing to say," Mama Dean said.

"It's only the truth. Toy did leave home, but only for a few hours. She got fed up with Bobby treating her like a doormat."

I'd rolled the top of Mama Dean's hair, now I was sectioning off the sides. The radio was playing "On The Rock Where Moses Stood."

"It's always over some stinking man. But now Toy's gone and ruint herself. And her with that new ranch-style house with the automatic garage door opener. I tell you, the women's getting as selfish and no-account as the men," Mama Dean said.

"Toy's not selfish and no-account. If anything she was too nice for her own good," I said.

"Well, she couldn't be *that* nice or she'd stay at home. A real mother's place is at home with her children, not gallivanting off to some art school. If her nerves is bad let her take up something soothing like cake-decorating or crocheting, something for the family. She could even start a ceramics shop in her garage and never have to go anywhere," Mama Dean said.

"Ceramics would go good here in Poplar Grove. The ceramics shop in Harmony is so busy people have to take numbers to use the kiln," Mother said.

"Mrs. Babcock from our church goes over there. She made those cute little frogs with fishing-poles. Why, she's made gnomes, dozens of the prettiest things," Mama Dean said.

"But Toy doesn't want ceramics, she wants art school," I said.

"Hmph. Art school don't put food on the table. It's as useless as tits on a bull," Mama Dean said.

"Lord, Mama Dean! It doesn't matter if everyone thinks it's useless, it's what Toy wants. While Toy was nicing-herself-to-death, Bobby was doing exactly what he wanted and no one ever accused him of not being a 'real' father. I don't see why she can't do what she wants instead of doing what she has to do and pretending it's what she wants," I said.

"Well, Maggie Sweet!"

"Well, it's true. Can't Toy have a life? Isn't she a person? Look what all Mary Price has done and she's..."

"Mary Price is entirely different. She was always different. Hoyt knew that before he married her. Bless his heart. But Toy changed *after*. A person can't go around changing *after*. Why, just think how Bobby and those children must feel with Toy going around like a hippie," Mama Dean said.

"You don't have to bless Hoyt's heart. He's not pitiful." My neck felt hot. It's true what they say about getting hot under the collar.

"What did you say, Maggie Sweet?" Mama Dean said.

"I said Hoyt isn't pitiful. They might fuss and argue but at least they know they're alive," I said.

"We're not talking about Hoyt and Mary Price. We're talking about people changing *after*. People ought *not* to change after they marry."

I didn't think, I just blurted out, "Well, for goodness

sake, Mama Dean. If people can't change after, they might as well book the church for their wedding and funeral on the same day—cut out the middle fifty years altogether."

Mama Dean just looked at me. Then she said, "Speaking of people changing *after*. I heard you was seen dancing in the Winn-Dixie a while back. There's some that says you must've been drinking the way you was carrying on."

I took a deep breath. I'd taken the bait, walked right into her trap after all.

"Well, damn! Damn that Dreama Nims, anyway," I flared.

"Well, sister! What a thing to say!" Mama Dean said.

"Maggie Sweet, there's no need to cuss," Mother said.

"It's enough to make a preacher cuss, Mother! Dreama Nims talking about me to my own grandmother. I can't believe it!"

Mama Dean narrowed her eyes to slits. "What I want to know, sister is: is it true?"

"Lord, Mama Dean, I *was* dancing. Mary Price and Hoyt were in the Winn-Dixie...they'd just found out they had the job at the Palomino. We were laughing, hugging...celebrating. I tell you, I could kill Dreama Nims!"

"They say the boy you dated back in school was in on it," Mama Dean went on, dismissing my explanation like a dog flicking off a flea.

My eyes welled up. Mama Dean knew about Jerry!

Nobody said anything for a while.

Finally, Mother said, "Now, Mama, there's no need of this. Nobody was 'in on' anything. Nothing happened. Why, that boy was twenty years ago. Besides, Maggie

Sweet doesn't drink or gallivant. She'd never do a thing in this world to shame any of us. She's been a good wife and mother, you've said so yourself a million times. She even gave up that beauty shop she wanted so bad to stay home with her children."

Mother defending me made me feel worse than Mama Dean fussing at me. Her absolute belief that I'd always do the right thing made my stomach clench and my eyes well up, but so far, it had always worked.

"I didn't give it up, Mother. Steven wouldn't let me work," I muttered.

"And I thank God every day for that," Mother said. "Steven's a good man. I'd have given anything to have stayed home and raised you full time."

"But my girls are raised. What am I supposed to do now?"

"See, Betty. I told you she bears watching. And sister, I can sure as the world tell you what you're *not* supposed to do." Mama Dean shook her finger at me.

I ducked my head. Felt the tears behind my eyes.

"Lord, Mama," Mother said. "Life's hard on women and Maggie's always been deep. Why, I've seen her staring out the window up the road for years. But she'd never go back on her raising. She's always done the right thing. And I know she'll do the right thing now."

Oh, Lord.

"Hmmph. Hard times! Hard times. You all don't know a thing about hard times. Why, Maggie's got every-thing a body could want, a family, a fine home in the historical part of town, that add-a-pearl necklace...I don't know what more she could want. I'll tell you about hard times; the Depression was hard times, walking to school barefoot, living off corn bread and beans. Why, I could go on and on."

I wanted to say, I know you've seen hard times, but it's hard to turn an add-a-pearl necklace into a reason for living. But I kept quiet. Mama Dean was still going "on and on" when I covered her curlers with a net and tucked her under the dryer.

Lying in bed with Jerry that afternoon, I told him about Dreama's gossip and what Mother and Mama Dean had said.

"You've got to tell them, honey. It'll be a lot easier when you tell them you're leaving, when everything's out in the open." he said.

"How can I leave now? The girls graduate in two weeks."

We'd talked about me leaving, almost nothing else, since that first day. But I'd never really thought it through. Somehow I just pictured it happening: Maggie and Jerry living happily ever after at the farmhouse. Wave a magic wand, wish upon a star, blow out your birthday candles and make your dreams come true. But I'd never thought about the actual steps; the actual *telling*.

How would I tell them? Call a family meeting, announce it to all the relatives over Sunday dinner? Tell them at the graduation party? I could bring it up casually while Steven carved the ham. "Oh, by the way. I'm moving out right after dinner. But you all take your time. Don't worry about a thing. The U-Haul won't be here 'til after dessert."

Would my motherless daughters' lips tremble over the potato salad? What about Mama Dean's tragic broken figure, the hurt in Mother's eyes, Daddy and Willa Mae's embarrassment, Mother Presson's sinking spell? What would Steven do? In spite of everything, he was clueless. He seemed to think we'd limp along side by side 'til All Souls Cemetery and eternity.

Could I wait 'til he was asleep, leave a note, slip off in the dead of night—the coward's way out?

But for some reason, even more than telling Steven and the girls, I dreaded telling Mother and Mama Dean.

"Oh, Lord! They think my whole life's settled— that I'll always do the right thing. They see me as this good..."

Jerry sighed. "Lord, Maggie, you sound like you did back in school. I thought you were past that."

"Well, I guess I have lost my 'good girl' standing," I said, covering myself with the queen-size sheet. "But everything I've ever known is flashing before my eyes. I just...I don't know how to do this."

Jerry sat up, pulled on his clothes and left the room.

I wrapped the sheet around myself and followed him.

In the kitchen, he kept his back to me as he scooped coffee into a filter. He looked calm, but the set of his back said pure tight-lipped Navy.

"Tell me what you're thinking. Don't shut me out if you're mad," I said.

"I'm not mad. It's just...God, Maggie. We knew it wouldn't be easy. I keep thinking about what happened to us back in school. You wouldn't stand up for yourself then and you can't stand up for yourself now."

"That's not fair. It's only been a few weeks. I need time to work everything out. You said yourself that it'd be a mess, that I was the one with everything to lose. I just want everyone to be all right," I said.

He stared past me, out the window. Then his

shoulders slumped. "Yeah. You're right. I *am* rushing you. It's just—for a minute there, it was like we'd had this exact conversation before." He shook his head to clear it. "Do you remember the first time we were together here at the farmhouse? You asked me if I thought two seventeen year olds could have been in love for real—could have been each other's real life? Do you understand how lucky we are to have found each other again? How special it is to get another chance? I know it won't be easy, but we can't let that stop us. Don't you see, Maggie, this might be the last chance we get."

He got up and poured coffee strong enough to walk to the table by itself. When he'd made the coffee, he'd forgotten to measure. He hadn't been calm and collected after all.

"We're not seventeen anymore, Maggie. We'll never see our golden wedding anniversary. I want us to walk through town holding hands—to get started."

"Do you really think they'll be all right?"

"They'll be fine, honey. They'll be better than fine," he said.

I reached for his hand. "If I tell them as soon as the girls graduate, we'll only be eighty-eight on our golden wedding anniversary."

Chapter Seventeen

The next week, when I wasn't with Jerry, I concentrated on the girls' graduation party. For months, I'd been stocking up on cake mixes and confectioner's sugar, macaroni, pickles, mayonnaise and mustard, Jello and canned fruit for salads, a fancy paper table cloth and napkins, candles, butter mints, nuts, and ingredients for the punch. Wednesday, I bought a twenty-pound ham on sale at Winn-Dixie.

I'd just wrestled the ham into the kitchen when Jill came up behind me.

"Hey, Mama."

"Lord, Jill. You scared me to death! I thought you were in school!"

"I've got...uh...cramps. The school nurse tried to call you."

I gave her Midol and the heating pad and she went back to bed. Then, I carried the ham down the basement stairs and put it in the deep-freeze and went back upstairs to check on Jill. She was in her room with the phone cord stretched under her door.

Starting toward her room, I heard, "You've got to see me...no, I haven't seen a doctor...I just *know*. You said you'd take care of it! All right, I'll see you at three."

I stopped dead in my tracks, my heart pounding like a hammer. I cannot tell you all the thoughts in my head.

A second later she came out in the hall and saw me standing there. We stared at each other for a full minute. It was awful.

Finally Jill said, "You scared me to death. I thought you were downstairs."

"Who were you talking to?"

"When?" she asked, pale and shifty-eyed.

"Just now. On the phone. I heard you."

"You shouldn't have been listening in on me! What did you hear?" She was trying to turn it around, like I'd done something wrong.

"We can stand here all day if you want to, but you *will* tell me."

"Nothing's going on. Why can't you leave me alone?"

"I'm your mother. I'm not going to leave you alone."

"Don't start that 'talk to me, I'm your mother' stuff. You always say that but when I tell you anything you get upset. Besides, it's my body and I'll do what I want with it." She prissed past me into her room and shut the door.

I barged in behind her. I didn't even bother to knock. Her saying "my body" made the hair on my neck stand straight up. "Don't you slam your door on me. Tell me what's going on."

"All right! If you really want to know, I'll tell you. In fact, I'll show you!" She turned around and dropped her jeans.

For a minute I got swimmy-headed.

Jill had a tattoo on her butt—an eagle tattoo!

"Are you happy now?" she wailed. "Oh, Mama, I think it's infected! Gangrene's setting in."

I stood there with my mouth dropped open and my

stomach heaving. I didn't know what to do. Part of me wanted to hug her 'cause it wasn't any of the terrible things I'd been thinking, but I also wanted to hit her 'cause *hotalmightydamn!* my own little girl had a tattoo on her butt!

"Lord, Jill! When did you do this?"

"Friday."

I thought back to Friday. I'd gone to Chatham Road that day. If I'd been home, it might not have happened. Then I thought, Jill should have been in school on Friday. "So you played hooky, too?" I said.

"It doesn't matter. I've got all the credits I need so they have to give me my diploma. Besides, I'm not going to graduation and I'm not going to college, either. I'm taking carving classes from the chief and that's all there is to that." She crossed her arms over her chest and glared at me like Mama Dean.

I couldn't believe it! She was going to stand there and get snippy with me, talk back to me when she had a tattoo! I pinched her, hard, on the arm.

She looked shocked. "God, Mama, that hurt!"

"If you say another word about graduation, I swear I'll pinch your head off. I shudder to think what your daddy will say about all this."

Her face went white as flour. "Why do you have to tell Daddy?"

This went right through me. It didn't matter one almighty bit what I thought, but let her Daddy get mad and she went all to pieces. "I have to tell him. You can't go around doing anything you take in your head to do."

She started to cry. "But, he's always mad at me. It's like I had to do something he'd hate to get back at him."

"You can't go around disfiguring yourself to get back

at people."

"I know it was stupid. But it seemed like a good idea at the time," she said, sounding like she did at two.

I checked the tattoo. It wasn't infected, only new and tender. I thought of infection, blood-poisoning, my daughter paying cash money to get herself disfigured for life. For a minute I thought I might vomit.

I got the First-Aid kit from the medicine cabinet, found the tube of Neosporin, and handed it to Jill. I was too queasy to dab it on myself.

By then I was so dizzy, I had to lie down. I went to my room and thought about Steven and Jill. It was true, they did nothing but fuss and argue now. If I told Steven about the tattoo it would only get worse. Steven'd have a hissy. Jill would stomp out the door. On the other hand, if I didn't tell him and he found out...I tried not to think about that. How much of this was my fault? Would it have made any difference if I'd been home that day?

I got up, went down the hall to Jill's room. She looked miserable. I sat on the edge of her bed. "I've decided not to tell Daddy."

"Thanks, Mama," she said, her eyes full.

"Don't thank me yet. You've got to go to graduation—behave yourself. We can't be having World War III around here all the time."

"I know. But the rules around here are so stupid." She leaned on her elbow and studied me. "Why's Daddy mad all the time?"

"He's not mad at you. He's mad at me because of Palomino Joe's."

"That was ages ago. If he's still mad over that, he'll never get over me not going to college."

"Jill..."

"I'm not going, Mama. I plan to carve. People say I'm good. I've got to see what I can do. Daddy makes everything so hard. Why can't he just let me be?"

I started to say "it's for your own good." But I stopped myself. Was going to college really for Jill's good, or was it just what was expected of Steven Presson's daughter? I thought back twenty years, when my family had shipped me off to Chapel Hill, changed my life forever, for my own good. Maybe if they'd let me be, I'd be married to Jerry now and running "Styles By Maggie Roberts" instead of sneaking around, trying to fix my eighteen-year-old life.

Oh, Lord. What we did to the people we loved for their own good.

That afternoon, when Jill went out to the garage workshop, I drove to the pay phone at Dixie Burger. "I'm sorry about today, honey. Jill's been home all day. I'm calling from a pay phone."

"Sick?"

"Not exactly. I don't want you to think bad of her...but she got this tattoo..."

"Tattoo?"

"An eagle tattoo on her...well...I couldn't leave. It was awful. She thought it was infected and got all torn up. Then I got torn up. She says she's not going to college no matter what. Steven'll have a hissy when everything hits the fan."

"Slow down, honey. Did you say a tattoo?"

"Let's not talk about it anymore. You didn't cook did you?"

"I marinated steaks all night."

Jerry always cooked for us, marinated steaks, blackened fish, key-lime pie; foods I'd never heard of. Then he served them all man-style, right from the pan.

"I'm sorry. Seem's all I ever say is 'sorry'."

"Don't worry, honey. The steak'll keep. And don't worry about Jill. From everything you've said, I like her. She just had a dumb-ass attack. Seems to go with the territory. So many attacks per teen. Did I ever tell you about the dumbest thing I did in my teens?"

"Does it have anything to do with me?"

"It has everything to do with you."

"Tell me again."

"Tomorrow?"

"Tomorrow."

Chapter Eighteen

There was either a full moon, or Mama Dean was right, the world was going downhill in a hand-basket.

I was driving down East Main Street, on my way to the farmhouse, when I saw a FOR SALE sign in front of The Curl & Swirl. I like to have crashed my car through Shirley's plate glass window when I saw it.

I parked the car and went inside. Shirley was at her appointment desk, under a set of wind chimes, dabbing her eyes with a Kleenex. When she saw me, she gave me a quivering grin and said, "Lord, Maggie. I didn't plan to get caught like this. The realtor just left and I'm having a squalling spell. I'm almost through. It's only a mini-squall."

"Oh, Shirley, I didn't know," I said, close to having a spell of my own.

"I've decided to sell the place, get a condo at the beach. Quit while my legs are still good enough for a bathing suit." She hiked up her pant leg to show-off a muscular calf in orange support hose. Then she picked up a mirror and scrubbed at the smudged mascara under her eyes. "Lordymercy, I'm a mess. Reckon I better fix up this face or go down to the pound and apply for a dog license."

I knew she expected me to laugh, but her trying to joke at a time like this only made me feel worse. I ached to hug her. There were a thousand things I wanted to say. But she was making it clear that the last thing she wanted was a fuss. She wanted me and everyone else to think she was shrugging off The Curl & Swirl with a wink and a wisecrack as if it wasn't breaking her heart. I gathered myself. If I said the wrong thing, made one false move, she'd go all to pieces and embarrass herself to death.

While she concentrated on her makeup, I thought about making an excuse and slipping out the door to give her time to pull herself together. Then I heard another set of wind chimes and Mrs. Mabes, Shirley's mother, came out of the back room carrying a coffee pot.

"Hey, Maggie," she said.

"Hey, Mrs. Mabes."

Mrs. Mabes handed us Styrofoam cups of coffee, gave the wind chimes a look that should have frozen them into silence forever, then glared at Shirley. "Maggie Sweet, I want you to talk some sense into Shirley. She's letting them aliens run her out of town."

Shirley set down the mirror and rolled her eyes at me. "Mama calls the people at the Beauty Box 'aliens'. She calls everyone who wasn't born in Poplar Grove aliens. But they're not running me off. Retiring to the beach isn't exactly a punishment from God, Mama."

"Why, I wouldn't go to the beach to see Jimmy Carter himself," Mrs. Mabes snorted.

Shirley stirred her coffee and sighed. "I can't tell you how thrilled I am to be discussing this for the millionth time this week. Mama thinks I'm giving up, not retiring. She thinks I ought to go out kicking and screaming."

Mrs. Mabes looked at me. "I tell you kicking and screaming's the only way to go. Before I'd let them aliens run me out of town, I'd advertise more, run more specials, load the seniors from the Methodist Home on a bus and drive them down here myself if I had to. We was here first. I sure as the world wouldn't roll over and play dead for no aliens."

"I'm not playing dead, Mama. We've had a good run. Now it's over."

"We could give door prizes, put in a tanning bed, give bikini waxes..." Mrs. Mabes went on, talking right over Shirley.

Shirley shook her head. "Hope springs eternal for Mama. 'Course she also believes that big hair and beehives are making a comeback."

"It could happen. Stranger things than that have happened," Mrs. Mabes said.

"Lord, Mama, you're just being stubborn. We've hung on too long as it is. From the minute the Beauty Box moved into the mall, it was meant to be. Our fate was sealed. It was in the stars. Part of some universal plan. Now it's time to quit, to let it go," Shirley said, twirling her crystal pendant absentmindedly.

"Bullshit and applesauce! That's universal hogwash and you know it! I didn't raise my daughter to be no quitter."

"You didn't raise me to be a fool, either, Mama. Now let's stop this fussing. Maggie didn't come here to listen to us fuss."

"Well, pardon me for speaking. I'm just as universally sorry as I can be," Mrs. Mabes pulled herself up stiffly, gave the wind chimes a jerk, and hobbled to the back room.

After she left, we sat there a while, not saying anything.

Finally, Shirley said, "Lord, Maggie, I'm sorry you had to witness this mess."

"She's just upset."

"Don't I know it. We've been fussing like this for weeks. I know it's hurt Mama—hurt her to the core. But I didn't plan to go out like this either. I've done all I know to do and more. But, I swanee, I'm still eat up with guilt like a dog's eat up with mange."

I thought about Shirley and Mrs. Mabes, how The Curl & Swirl had been passed down from mother to daughter like farm land being passed down from father to son. Mrs. Mabes had started it before World War II with money borrowed from her mother. In the late fifties, Shirley had taken it over and turned it into the busiest shop in town. Now, after all these years, Shirley was the one to lose it. No wonder she felt awful.

"There's got to be another way," I said.

"We've been dead as a hammer for two years."

"What would it take to turn things around?" I asked.

"Vidal Sassoon...an accident at the Beauty Box involving kerosene and a match. Any way you slice, it'd take a miracle."

"There's got to be something..."

"I've turned it over and over in my mind for months," she said.

"Maybe you could find some young stylist in Charlotte. Bring her here. Offer that cute apartment in the back...you know, a package deal. Why, anyone starting out would be lucky to have..."

"I've tried that. I've gone as far away as Atlanta. But they'd take one look at our big-hair, tight-perm clients and say, 'Sorry, Shirley, I'm gone.' Times have changed, Maggie. Use to, a young stylist would be thrilled to have a set-up like this. But nowadays they don't see it as a place to start. They see it as a career move—a bad career move. They figure if they're seen in my shop, their reputation as an up-and-coming stylist would be ruined before it got started. Next thing I know they've signed on at the Beauty Box or they've caught the first bus back to Atlanta."

"Why don't you take some classes? They're bound to have refresher courses now that short-dos have made a comeback," I said.

"I tried. I can cut hair 'til the cows come home, but these precision cuts are tricky. I just can't seem to get the hang of 'em. Guess you can't teach an old dog new tricks. I need to face it, I'm precision-cut illiterate."

"Lord, Shirley, I wish there was something I could do."

"I wish that husband of yours had let you work here. You'd have a big following by now. We could've given the Beauty Box a real run for its money. But there's no use crying over split Dippity-Do."

Shirley and I had talked about my following, where the shop would be if I'd started working right out of beauty school. I thought about my plan to leave Steven. I'd need a job, a place to live. It would be perfect.

"What if I said I could come to work now? That I *want* to work," I said, my voice rising. I'd daydreamed about this moment for years.

Shirley didn't even look up. She sipped her coffee and stared off into space. Finally she said, "Law me, I'd love to have you here, just for the company. But there's no use breaking up your happy home over a lost cause. Besides, even if you started this very day, it's too late. No one comes to The Curl & Swirl looking for modern cuts. You'd just be standing around, wasting your time. I've already had to cut Dixie and Lurleen's hours to the bone. But, thanks, Maggie. I appreciate the offer."

We sat there drinking coffee, not speaking. Shirley

didn't believe I wanted to work. She thought I was just being nice, saying the right thing to cheer her up. I considered telling her I'd be needing a job, that she'd be doing me the favor. But it didn't seem right since I hadn't told my family I was leaving.

Now I wondered what I'd do. I'd taken for granted The Curl & Swirl would be waiting for me when I got ready. Now that I was ready it was too late.

Cutting hair was the only thing I was qualified to do. The only thing I wanted to do. I wouldn't work at the Beauty Box out of loyalty to Shirley, and the next nearest shop was thirty miles away (too far for my old car to travel).

I saw myself working in the Zippy Mart, wearing a blue smock with the name MAGGIE emblazoned on the pocket. I'd emboss credit cards, turn hot dogs on a rotisserie, pour syrup into a Slurpee machine, say "Y'all come back," a thousand times a day from behind my bullet-proof shield. Oh, no!

I thought about the Methodist home. They were always giving nurse's aide courses. I'd pass dinner trays and bed pans, learn to give back rubs, move on to bed baths and Fleet enemas. Oh, Lord!

We sat there for a long time, lost in our own thoughts. I didn't leave 'til the wind chimes announced the first customers: ninety-something Mrs. Gentry and her sister, Mrs. Lovelace. Mrs. Gentry wore a blue-rinsed tight perm and Mrs. Lovelace's hair was so thin, you could set it all in one pincurl.

When I said good-bye, Shirley shrugged her shoulders and gave me a tired I-told-you-so wink.

All the way to the farmhouse, I thought about the

generations of women who'd come through Shirley's doors—regulars with weekly standing appointments, women who came for only the most special events of their lives like weddings and graduations. I'd spent my teens there—taken for granted I'd spend my grown-up years there, too. Now, any hope of that was gone. It was the end of an era, the end of a dream.

As I drove down Chatham Road toward the farm-house, I saw Jerry riding his John Deere, an acre away. I waved, pulled my car behind an out building, and let myself into the house.

Going through to the kitchen, I was in such a fog, I barely noticed the newspapers strewn on the front room couch, the cups on the coffee table where we'd left them two days before.

I rinsed out the coffee pot, measured coffee into a filter, almost bumping into a ladder that had been left in the middle of the room. Dirty dishes were stacked in the sink. I washed two mugs, half-saw the empty Miller Draft six-pack on the counter. If I hadn't been so dazed, I'd have noticed that the whole house was messy and cluttered, very unlike everything-in-its-place Jerry. But with my mind on The Curl & Swirl, the house barely registered.

By the time Jerry came in, the coffee was brewing. He gave me a quick, sweaty kiss, said, "I'll be back as soon as I shower." Then he disappeared down the hall to the bathroom.

Somewhere in the back of the house, a radio played Willie Nelson's "Blue Eyes Crying In The Rain."

Deep in thought, I sat on the couch, drank coffee, and waited.

A few minutes later, he was back, smelling of soap and shampoo, dressed in clean jeans and a white T, his feet bare, his wet hair slicked back. He went to the kitchen, then carried his coffee mug to a chair six feet away.

"I'd have been here earlier, but I stopped at Shirley's. You'll never guess..." I started.

"I've got to go to Florida for a few days," he said.

"What?" With all that was on my mind, I wasn't sure I'd heard him right.

"I've got to go to Jacksonville. I'm flying out this afternoon."

"I thought the date for your final decree wasn't 'til next week."

"Yeah...that's another thing." He looked past me, out the window. For the first time I noticed how tired he looked.

"What's going on?"

"Trey's in a mess, had one of his dumb-ass attacks."

"There's a lot of that going around," I said, watching his face, keeping my voice steady.

"Yeah. But this one landed him in the brig."

"Oh, no, what happened?"

"He got knee-walking drunk, was late getting back from leave, got his ear pierced..."

"Oh, Lord!" I thought about all the messes Jill got into, how her worst punishment was being grounded for a week. "Couldn't they talk to him...give him a warning? I mean, the brig, my Lord!"

He stiffened. "Look, Maggie, Trey's in the Navy, not some Sunday school sleep-away camp. He deliberately broke regulations."

When had my outlaw got so righteous, so rule-abiding? He'd spent his teens breaking rules. *We* were breaking all the rules just being together.

"How can you say that? When did rules and regulations ever make a damn to you?" I flared.

He turned, his eyes blazing. "My son makes a damn to me! I didn't make the rules and regulations—the Navy did. Trey had choices, but he chose the Navy. Now they own his butt for the next four years. Like it or not, he can go along quietly, maybe learn something, or he can fight every rule that comes down the pike and make it four years of misery."

He stopped talking. Silence fell between us. I'd never seen him like this before. For the first time ever, it hit me: for twenty years we'd had completely separate lives. He'd talked about his son, his almost-ex-wife, but I'd never seen them as real people. I'd never thought of Jerry's life apart from me as real, never imagined his years of struggle, arguing with his wife, following Navy regulations, raising his son to have an easier life than his. Somehow, I'd seen him looking out a window or reading a book (daydreaming about me?) while his life happened around him.

Now, I saw his life had been as tangled as mine with worry and duty and trying to do the right thing. Except in my daydreams that other life had nothing to do with me.

My face burned with shame. "I'm sorry. I didn't think..."

We drank coffee, stared past each other; close at hand, just out of reach.

Then I remembered. "You said there was another thing?"

"I didn't want to tell you...but Brenda's been calling."

"But I thought..."

"I thought so, too. Then, all this mess with Trey—she called me again last night."

"Will you have to see her?"

"God, Maggie, our son's in the brig. She's a wreck."

"There's more, isn't there?" I breathed in and out, shut my eyes and opened them. All the air seemed to have left the room.

"Yeah. She's having second thoughts."

"About you?"

"Yeah. The single life isn't what she thought it'd be; she probably wants more money or something. She laid this whole guilt-trip on me, said Trey never had any problems until we split...said it wasn't too late...our divorce isn't final."

Oh Lord.

He stopped pacing, stared out the window awhile, then flopped back into the chair. "God, this has thrown me completely. I thought this part was settled...but she sounded so desperate. She was crying."

I bit my lip. For the second time that morning, I was close to crying myself. "The girls graduate next week. I'd planned to tell everyone. What do you want me to do?"

"You better hold off a while. I don't know what I'll find when I get down there."

"Will you call me?"

"If I can."

"What do you mean 'if'?" He still hadn't looked at me. I was trying not to feel deep down hurt.

"If I can," he said, exasperated.

I crossed the room, sat on the arm of his chair. He didn't reach for me, didn't even see me. Emmy Lou Harris was singing "Making Believe That You Still Love Me." We sat there for what seemed like hours. We'd been six feet apart, now we were miles apart. Emmy Lou's plans for the future would never come true, making believe was all she could do. Tears gathered behind my eyes. I stood and picked up my purse. He didn't try to stop me.

"If I don't hear from you, give Brenda my best, and have a good life," I said.

He looked stunned. "Dammit, Maggie, that's not fair."

I stumbled to my car. We were still on the same wavelength. Not fair, was exactly what I was thinking.

My stomach lurched as I barreled down the driveway, then onto Chatham Road, past Belews Pond. I was scared to death. It didn't help that Elvis, out of all the songs he knew, picked just then to sing, "Are You Lonesome Tonight." I clicked off the radio. What if he didn't want me? What if he wanted to put "The End" to the Maggie-Jerry story, stay in Jacksonville, go back to them? Oh, God! It'd be just like him. He'd see the pain in Brenda's eyes, his son's confusion; he'd decide he owed it to them to stay. I loved him because his feelings ran so deep, because he wasn't afraid to look into someone's eyes and see the pain and confusion there. Now, the thing I loved about him most was the very thing that was taking him away from me.

Nothing had changed since high school. I had lost him then, I was losing him now. There wasn't a thing I could do to stop it.

I pulled over to the side of the road, had a good cry, rolled down the window, breathed a little.

Then it hit me: I was doing what I'd done back in school. I was giving him up, letting other people come between us. There wasn't much else I could have done back then, but I wasn't a helpless school girl anymore. I understood his worry about his son, but when he'd talked about Brenda, I'd panicked. Jerry had warned me that it would be a mess. Now that it was getting messy, I'd stomped off.

He'd told me that I was the one with everything to lose, but what had it cost him when I'd canceled our plans at the last minute because of Jill or Mama Dean? How had he felt when I'd gone home to my family every night, lived a regular life, slept in my husband's bed? What had gone through his mind while he'd waited alone at the farmhouse?

I thought about how small and stunted my life had been without him, how I'd spent most of it sleepwalking. Why was I barreling down the road, rushing back to that old, dead life when my real life was at the farmhouse?

So what if it was messy and scary and complicated? None of that mattered. All that mattered was that Jerry was the center of my life. Whatever happened, I'd always love him. When I thought about life without him I felt bleak and hopeless and filled with regret. I could lose him anyway, but if I didn't go back, didn't see this through, I'd have to live with those feelings forever, always wondering if it was my fault.

I took a deep breath and did the only thing I could do: I made a wide U-turn and barreled back up the road to the farmhouse.

He met me at the door. For a minute we just stood there. Then we fell into each others arms and held on tight.

"God," he said. "When you drove down the driveway and never looked back, I thought it was over."

"I panicked. When you said you'd call 'if' you could, I thought you didn't want to...that you wanted it over. That going to Jacksonville meant..."

"How could you think that? I *want* to call you. But I don't even know where I'll be. I'll be tied up with the lawyers, visiting Trey, trying to reason with Brenda—and I can only call you when your family's not there."

Once again my face burned with shame. "Oh, Lord. I'm sorry. I guess the trouble with me is I could never believe in my good luck."

After that we didn't talk anymore. We just held onto each other 'til it was time for him to go.

Chapter Nineteen

All day Saturday, I brooded around the house, chain-smoked in the basement, and jumped out of my skin every time the phone rang.

Then, Sunday, I decided that full-moon, half-moon or no moon at all, the girls' graduation was still Friday. I put myself back on automatic-pilot and went through the motions, my body in Poplar Grove, my head and heart in Jacksonville.

By Monday night, the house was spotless. The freezer was loaded with pies, a chocolate sheet cake, green bean and broccoli casseroles, and containers of rice.

When Steven came home after one of his meetings, he took one look at all the food and muttered, "Dammit, Maggie. How much have you spent on this party?"

A few months ago this would have upset me something awful. But this time the oddest thing happened. I looked at him and I thought, who in the world are you? I don't know you. We'd been together for nineteen years, but he didn't seem to have anything to do with me. It was as if a stranger had accidentally taken a wrong turn and ended up in my kitchen.

This feeling hit me so hard, I had to look away so he wouldn't see the shock on my face.

But he must have sensed something. Because, after that, he stayed in the den grading finals while I stayed in the rest of the house. At meals we'd eat without a word, like two strangers in a diner.

At least I didn't have to worry about sex. I didn't know what I'd do if he wanted sex.

All week I ran back and forth to the boarding house borrowing Mother and Mama Dean's punch bowl and cups, extra folding chairs and the good lace tablecloth. Mama Dean insisted on making a Harvey Wallbanger cake, which we really didn't need. But I didn't have the energy to argue.

Wednesday morning, on the way home from the boarding house, I stopped off at The Curl & Swirl to invite Shirley and her mother to the girls' party.

The last person I expected to see at Shirley's was Dreama Nims. I'd avoided her since she'd gossiped to Mama Dean—hoped to avoid her forever. But there she sat, big as life, with Shirley teasing her hair so high she'd need a step-stool to touch it up.

"Hey, Maggie Sweet," she said. "I was just telling Shirley about the reunion. Looks to me like everyone and their sister will be there. Do you remember Ruby Poteet and Earline Sikes? They're *grandmothers*! Do you believe it? Thirty-eight years old and already *grandmothers*."

"That makes me feel old, old, old," Shirley said.

"Hmm," was all I could manage.

"Well, they are mighty young for grandmothers. But they were mighty young mothers, too. They got married in the eleventh grade. Had to, you know," Dreama said.

"That was over twenty years ago, Dreama. I guess they've paid their debt to society by now," I muttered.

Dreama was watching herself so closely in the mirror that I wondered if she'd heard me. By now her hair was piled up so high she'd need a ladder to comb it. But she glared at Shirley and said, "I told you, I want it fuller. I've got a big week planned, what with Dreama, Jr. graduating and all, and I don't want it going flat on me. Use plenty of that hair spritz."

Shirley clenched her jaw, and kept teasing and spraying. The radio was playing "Love Will Turn You Around."

Dreama frowned in the mirror, turning her head this way and that. Finally, she said, "What were you saying, Maggie Sweet?"

I bit my tongue. "Nothing. Not a thing in this world."

"I heard you say something. Something about paying a debt to society..."

"I just think after twenty-odd years of good behavior, they shouldn't still have to go through life being called Ruby and Earline HADTOYOUKNOW!" I'd planned to stay calm, but suddenly I was all worked up.

Shirley looked at me.

Dreama frowned at her reflection. "I told you more hair spray! And not that cheap old kind, neither!"

Shirley looked like she was getting a migraine.

Dreama glared into the mirror until she was satisfied Shirley wasn't using the "cheap old kind." Then, she leaned back and said, "I don't know what you're getting so upset about, Maggie Sweet."

I sighed. "Let's just drop it, Dreama. All I meant was Ruby and Earline could have spent their whole lives being Mother Theresa and you'd still want their tombstones to say: Here Lies Mother Theresa - Humanitarian - Angel of Mercy - Patron Saint Of The Poor—'course she HAD TO, YOU KNOW. Like HAD TO was the only thing they did in their lives that mattered."

Dreama looked at me. "Well, Maggie Sweet, that's the craziest thing I ever heard. Everyone knows Ruby and Earline aren't a thing in this world like Mother Theresa. Why, they aren't even Catholic."

Then she turned back toward the mirror. "By all rights, I didn't have to invite them to the reunion. I mean, they did drop out of school in eleventh grade, what with HAVING TO and all. But, I told myself, Dreama, it's your Christian duty to let bygones be bygone, to forgive even if you can't forget."

"That's very generous of you, I'm sure, Dreama," Shirley said. Shirley's face was the color of her smock—hot pink.

"Well, s-o-m-e-b-o-d-y has to make the effort," Dreama said piously. Then she looked in the mirror. "Shirley! For heaven's sake! My hair's already flat as a flitter! How many times do I have to tell you? I want more teasing and more spray!"

For a second Shirley just stood there. Then, she picked up two cans of spritz and aimed them directly at Dreama.

"You want more spray! Well, you've got it!" She said, spraying 'til Dreama disappeared in a smog of spritz.

When the mist finally cleared, Dreama's face was Pepto-Bismal pink. She whipped off the plastic cap, flung it to the floor and got out of the chair. "For goodness sake, Shirley, you don't have to drown me! I've only kept coming here 'cause I felt sorry for you. But, if that's all the thanks I get, I'll be switching to the Beauty Box *immediately!*"

Shirley stood there with her hands on her hips. "That's the Beauty Box' problem. They'll be getting a sympathy card from me *immediately!* "

Dreama, who had started toward the door, stopped, spun around and narrowed her eyes. "I'll be calling my attorney, Shirley. That was nothing but pure-T assault. And Maggie Sweet, I'm so sorry Jerry went back to Jacksonville before the reunion. 'Course if I'm not badly mistaken you all have been having your own *private* reunion for months!"

After that, everything went crazy. Shirley picked up both cans of spritz and ran full tilt toward Dreama spritzing away for all she was worth. For a second Dreama just stood there, her mouth wide open. Then her eyes went big and she took off through the parking lot like a scalded dog.

Shirley and I watched out the window for a minute. Then Shirley brushed off her hands like she'd done a good day's work. "I've been wanting to do that for years," she said.

"For a minute, I thought we'd have to do CPR," I said, nervously.

"Guess I went a little crazy. But I'm not sorry."

"I know. Half of me wants to sing the 'Hallelujah Chorus', but the other half wants to curl up on the floor and squall," I said.

"We've all been licking her boots for years, scared to death that she'd ruin us with her mean mouth. Well, I've had it. If she wants to ruin us, she'll just have to ruin away," Shirley said.

I thought about Jerry and what Dreama had said, but the room started spinning and I had to sit down.

Shirley poured two glasses of iced tea and handed me one. "I know it's scary, but the more I think about it, you know, being ruint, totally deep-down, through and through ruint could be kind of freeing. I've swallowed my pride—tip-toed around Dreama for years and despised myself for trying to stay on her good side. The truth is she don't have a good side. Sooner or later I'd have crossed her. Call me crazy, but I figure I just got it over with."

"Oh, Lord. I wish I could see it that way," I said, feeling depressed.

"Well, poor Ruby and Earline never crossed her and it didn't slow her down a heartbeat. Toting-up people's sins is what she does. It was only a matter of time before she got around to us anyway. Do you remember Nicole Bennett?"

"Sure. Nicole graduated with me. She was Poplar Grove's answer to Joan Collins," I said.

"Wait'll I tell you what Dreama said about Nicole. Said Nicole was...uh...a Lebanese."

"That's silly. Nicole's Scotch-Irish like everybody else in town."

"That's what I said. But, Dreama said, 'Shirley, you just don't get it. Nicole's a Lebanese. You know. One of those women who...uh...like other women.'"

"For goodness-sake, Shirley. What did you say?"

"I told her I didn't believe it. But she said, 'When I called Nicole about the reunion she said she'd be bringing a friend. A woman friend. Asked me to make motel reservations for them. *Motel reservations*, mind you. Why, if she wasn't *that way*, why wouldn't she stay with her Mama like everyone else?'"

"She decided all that over a motel reservation?"

"Yep. So I said, now Dreama, that's simply not true. Even when Nicole was a girl she ordered all her clothes from Frederick's of Hollywood. I mean, if she was that way, she'd have ordered them from *Field and Stream* or something. It was all I could think of to joke her out of it."

"She's too stupid to understand sarcasm," I said.

"Yep. I might as well have saved my breath to dry my nail polish. She said, 'Shirley, I can't believe that you could be that naive. Don't you ever watch Phil Donahue or anything? Why, clothes from Frederick's of Hollywood don't mean a thing.'"

"Her mind's getting smaller and meaner every day," I said.

"It's so small now, I keep expecting it to roll out her ear. But, that's what I'm saying. Nicole never crossed Dreama. Why, the poor woman lives out-of-state. Dreama just likes to ruin people because she *can*."

Shirley leaned back in her chair. "I keep thinking about that poor old Bucky Nims. I mean, can you imagine living with Dreama? From morning 'til night all he hears is, 'Bucky Nims, were you born in a barn? All you do is sit around and nasty up the place. Bucky, you'll never amount to a hill of beans. Bucky Nims, don't you dare talk back to my child...'"

"I know. And Bucky is so good-hearted. I could never figure out why he married her in the first place."

"She picked him out and he was too nice to hurt her feelings. Next thing he knew his fate was sealed," she said.

"He'd niced-himself to death."

"Yep. You saying that reminds me of this book I read. This man kept saying that he'd killed himself at age nineteen. He hadn't really killed himself, of course. He'd just married at nineteen and the marriage wasn't going so good. The whole time I was reading that book, I kept thinking about Bucky being that man. Bucky Nims killed himself the day he married Dreama. Maybe if he'd gone a little crazy—gone and ruint himself, he'd be alive today."

When I got home, I was lower than low. I thought

about Jerry not calling, about Dreama plotting to ruin my life. When I remembered that Mother Presson was coming Thursday for the l-o-n-g graduation weekend, I got so depressed, I went down to the basement and chain-smoked 'til supper time.

Wednesday morning, I was sitting at the kitchen table, going over the party menu for the hundredth time and trying not to think about everything, when the telephone rang.

"You alone?" Jerry asked.

"Oh, Lord, I've been crazy to talk to you. I started to call the farmhouse a dozen times, then remembered... Where are you?"

"I'm nowhere. A pay phone off-base. I saw Trey."

"How's he doing?" I wondered if he'd also seen Brenda, but was afraid to ask.

"Shut-down, bummed-out. I expected it, but it made me feel..."

"Awful."

"Yeah."

"What about...everything else?"

"Bad."

"Bad?"

"Worse than bad."

"It couldn't get any worse?"

"Trust me. It gets worse. Do you want to know?"

"I want to know."

"She's giving me all kinds of flak."

"Is the court date still Friday?"

"She's talking about postponing. I think she's bluffing, probably holding out for more money. Who knows? I could never figure her out. She thinks and talks in a foreign language. I'll call you Friday."

"Oh, Lord. You can't! I'll have a house full of people—the girls' party..."

"Oh yeah, graduation...I forgot."

I could hear the pay phone's hum, traffic whizzing past. Jerry's voice was slipping away. I had this crazy feeling that he was slipping away, too.

"What happens now?" I asked, my voice snagging.

He sucked in his breath. "I can't think straight. This whole mess has my head spinning."

I took a deep breath. "Are *we* a mess?" I wanted him to say that everything was going to be all right—to lie if he had to.

"We figured it'd be over by Friday. I'd be free, you could tell them. But we're still flying blind with our fingers crossed. Yeah. I guess you'd have to say we're a mess."

The operator interrupted, "Your three minutes are up, sir. Please deposit..."

"Oh no!" I wailed.

"Damn. I gotta go, Maggie. I'm out of change."

Once again I felt him slipping away. We hadn't said anything. Not really. Why hadn't he said, I love you. Why hadn't I? I wanted to throw my head back and howl.

"Wait a minute, operator...Maggie, are you still there?"

"Still here," I cried.

"Listen, honey, we'll get past this. It'll be all right. It's gotta be all right..."

I sat there for a long time, listening to the line hum, before I hung up. I was still staring out the kitchen window, feeling lower than a well, when Mary Price came to the back door.

She'd been busy for weeks, so we hadn't seen each

other, even though we'd talked on the phone almost every day. She'd talked about Palomino Joe's, new songs she was trying out, her costumes. I'd talked about Shirley's closing, the graduation party—everything but Jerry. It felt too private, too important to talk about, even with Mary Price. Besides, I was afraid if I told her about us, she'd think I was a heathen.

Her first words, when she came in the door, were, "Lord, Maggie. You look like you've been drug through hell backward!"

I got busy pouring tea, slicing lemons, not trusting myself to speak.

But the minute I sat down, she drilled me with her eyes and said, "I hear the old boyfriend went to Jacksonville."

Suddenly, fat, salty tears were running down my face, soaking the front of my T-shirt and plopping onto the table.

"Jumping Jesus! I was afraid of that. You love him, don't you?"

I nodded, but the tears were coming too fast to say anything. I never knew there could be so many tears.

"Oh, Lord, Maggie, I'm so sorry. I didn't know love would make you so miserable."

"I didn't know I could feel like this. Didn't know I could have such feelings. One minute my eyes are welling up from pure gratitude for being alive. Then I'm bawling because he's gone—maybe forever. Oh, Mary Price, I don't know what's going to happen. Maybe it was just five minutes of wonder for a lifetime of pain. And everyone will hate me."

She patted my hand. "Hush now. You can't worry about what everyone thinks. You're not the first married woman to fall in love with another man. And you won't be the last. Why, I have days when I'd run off with the Jewel-Tea man if he talked nice to me. Now, dry your eyes," she said, handing me a letter that was postmarked Jacksonville, Florida.

I looked at her, then tore it open.

Dear Maggie Sweet,

It's almost midnight. I'm sitting in my motel room, thinking about you. I don't know what's going to happen. But suddenly I wanted to write something for you. I haven't felt like writing since high school. But, then no one has called me an outlaw-poet since high school. I'll send this through Mary Price and hope it won't be too awkward for you.

THE GIRL AT BELEWS POND

In a Chevy
overlooking Belews Pond
a boy and a girl
too young
give themselves
to time and light
for all of memory.

Then, torn by youth and rules
and small-town gossip
they drift apart
do the "right" thing
numb their senses
take up separate lives.

At mid-life,
in a kitchen
in Poplar Grove
they collide
and the universe shifts—shakes itself
—comes clear.
For, there, in her eyes
he finds his soul
where he'd left it,
with the girl at Belews Pond
Always remember. I loved you then. I love you now.
I'll ALWAYS love you.

Jerry

After I read it, I cried harder than ever.

Mary Price didn't say anything. She just got the box of Kleenex, laid the pack of Virginia Slims on the table next to me and sat with me 'til I calmed down.

Chapter Twenty

Graduation was Friday. Thursday afternoon, right after school, Steven planned to drive to Chapel Hill to pick up Mother Presson.

At three o'clock, I was slicing potatoes into a skillet, for an early supper, when Jill slammed into the kitchen.

"You can forget the whole graduation thing," she bawled. "I'm not graduating, I've been expelled." Then she ran upstairs to her room.

Before I could go after her, Amy banged into the room. "This time she's done it. She's disgraced us for life. I could die. I could just die."

"Amy, what in the world...?"

"God, Mama, it was awful! Jill and her sorry friends greased the school banisters and everyone was falling all over the place. Then they rigged up a shoe to make footprints everywhere—even on the ceiling. They took the vice-principal's Volkswagen apart and put it back together inside the school lobby..." Amy stopped mid-sentence, gave me a look that said all of this was my fault, and ran up the stairs to her room.

I started to go after her, but the telephone rang.

"Tell Jill to be there when I get home," Steven said, in the coldest voice I'd ever heard.

I hung up the phone and ran up the stairs feeling like the sky was falling.

When I got to Jill's room, she was sitting on her bed, hugging her pillow against her chest.

"Oh, Jill, what have you gone and done? You promised to behave."

"God, Mama. I was trying to enter into the spirit of things...I know it was stupid...but...everyone's carrying on like I killed someone."

Downstairs a door banged and Steven bellowed, "Jill? Maggie? I'm home."

For a second, Jill looked like a deer caught in headlights. Then, her eyes went flat.

Steven was coming through the front room heading toward the stairs, when I caught up with him.

"Where's Jill?"

"In her room. Oh, Steven, calm down before you go up there."

"Don't tell me to calm down. My own daughter's made me a laughingstock at school. I tell you I've had it this time. She can shape up or ship out."

"Please, Steven, get a hold of yourself."

He brushed past me toward the stairs, but the telephone rang in the kitchen and he froze. I ran to answer it.

"It's the principal, Mr. Fentress," I hissed, holding my hand over the receiver.

Steven glared at me, grabbed the phone and changed from Mr. Hyde into Dr. Jekyll, right before my eyes.

"Yes, Braxton. How may I help you?"

I held my breath, got busy wiping off the counter, pouring tea, trying to hear what they said. I couldn't make out the words, only the low rumble of Mr. Fentress' voice. And Steven had his back to me so I couldn't read his face.

Just when I thought I couldn't stand it another second, Steven said, "Thank you, Braxton, I appreciate your seeing it that way."

He hung up the phone and slid onto a kitchen chair. I carried tea to the table, stealing sideways peeks at him, searching for a clue. He sat there a minute, staring at the glass as if he'd never seen it before.

"For goodness sake, Steven! Tell me what he said!"

He blinked, then looked at me as if he'd never seen me before. "The school has decided to chalk it up to graduation-week-high-spirits since half the seniors were in on it. If they clean up their mess they'll be allowed to graduate."

"Oh, Steven. See? It wasn't just Jill. It was half of her classmates. It was just a group dumb-ass attack," I rattled on, light-headed with relief.

Steven looked at me like I had nine heads. "Just this once, Maggie, try not to be vulgar. *You* might be relieved, but Jill's not getting off that easily with me. I meant what I said. She can shape up or ship out. I won't have people talking about us. She's nothing but a juvenile delinquent and I told her so."

Up 'til then, I'd tried to see Steven's side, but the words 'juvenile delinquent' flew all over me. Jill was not a juvenile delinquent. A fart in a whirlwind, maybe, a thorn in his side, for sure, but *not* a juvenile.

"You called Jill a juvenile?"

I still could not believe it. Ever since the girls were born, Steven had lectured me about name-calling. Why, once when Jill was little, I was playing around and called her a little booger. Steven got all over me like white on rice. He said calling children names, even if you were fooling around, was the worst thing a person could do. He even read me a section out of a child psychology book that said,

"Name-calling is as bad as physical abuse. It can scar a child for life!"

'Course now that Steven was upset, it was all right to scar away.

"Jill is not a juvenile, and I do not appreciate you calling her one," I said.

"For God sake, Maggie! It's not juvenile, it's juvenile delinquent. Can't you say anything right? And don't defend her. You're always defending her. A lot of this is your fault. You've always encouraged her. You and your whole family have encouraged her to embarrass me to death."

I was already upset, so when he started in on my family, I really lost my temper.

"I'm sorry, Steven," I said, my voice as cold as ice. "I'm sorry if we embarrass you. If me and my family don't measure up to you and your family's standards. Your la de dah family who can't sit in a room together for more than five minutes and haven't so much as hugged each other in nineteen years."

"Don't change the subject. I tell you you've spoiled her, spoiled her to death."

Oh Lord. We'd been having this same argument about Jill her whole life. Even when she was a baby he'd say, "Don't pick her up every times she cries. Don't feed her but every four hours. You'll spoil her."

And I'd feel guilty as home-made sin wondering if he was right, if I was spoiling her.

But Jill was a prickly, colicky baby, jumpy as a cricket, flying into tantrums for no reason. How could I not pick her up? How could I let her scream for hours until the next feeding? Jill was different. She was different from Steven, different from me, different from Amy, who seemed to be born with the cool, dignified Presson standards.

There was a fierceness about Jill that scared me to death but filled me with wonder, too. I loved her fierceness.

She never saw any danger. She was always pitching herself off the edges of furniture or stair-steps, jumping into the deep ends of pools, sure that someone would be there to catch her. And mostly I did catch her. But what was I supposed to do? Let her fall or drown to teach her about caution? Teach her about rules? I'm her mother, for the Lordsake and a mother's job is to protect her children.

When I thought about Jill, I saw her with her head thrown back laughing, bright as new money, full of life and fun and down-to-earth sense.

Steven only saw her as a girl who broke the rules. His rules. Everybody's rules. He couldn't stand that. He thought she broke the rules out of meanness, to embarrass him. But Jill didn't seem to know there were long lists of rules, didn't know she was supposed to be silenced, withered by a look from Steven.

I tried to keep my mouth shut, but I couldn't.

"She's not spoiled. She's just different. But she's your daughter. Doesn't that count for something? Maybe if you hadn't stayed locked up in your damned old den all the time, making up lists of rules, worrying about what everyone else thinks of us, maybe if you'd been *part* of this family, you'd *know* your daughter—caught her doing something good instead of only noticing when she does something wrong. Dammit, Steven, you never notice any of us unless we break one of your almighty rules!"

Steven's face looked purple. For a second, I thought he might hit me. "Don't you *ever* talk to me like that! I tell you I won't have it. I won't have you contradicting me. I won't have the entire town talking about us. Do you understand?" Then he slammed the den door so hard the ancestors on their guy-wires rattled.

I stood there for a minute, feeling like all the air had been sucked out of the room. This had gone too far for a few pranks. But the argument wasn't about Jill. It had been building between us for years. Now the words had been said. We could never take them back or forget them.

After awhile, I gathered myself as best I could, and went upstairs to see about Jill.

She was standing beside her bed, emptying her dresser drawers into a duffel bag.

"Oh, Jill. Don't"

"I'm gone, Mama. Don't try to stop me."

"Things will calm down. It'll be all right. Mr. Fentress called. You can still graduate."

"It won't be all right. It'll never be all right. Even if I graduate I'm not going to college or computer school. Daddy will just keep yelling and you'll keep trying to save me. It'll just go on and on."

I put my arms around her. This was breaking my heart.

She stiffened. "Don't Mama. I've only stayed this long because of you. If I don't leave now, I'll never have a life. I'll be stuck right here, doing everything I hate... leading some boring life...this life that *he* picked...well, maybe that's all you ever expected, but I'm not like you. It's not going to happen to me."

I tried not to think about how Jill saw my life. Her saying, "Maybe that's all you ever expected," said it all. Suddenly, I wanted to tell her that I wasn't just her timid little Mama. I still had hopes and dreams. I planned to run off with an outlaw poet, a man I'd loved since before she was born. I wanted to say that I'd be living at his home-place out in the country and she'd be welcome any time; that soon, very soon, I'd have something to offer her—a place to stay—an out building for her carving.

And if Jerry wasn't still in Jacksonville, if I'd already told Steven, if I was sure of anything in this world working out, I'd have told her. Instead, I said, "You can't go running off in the dead of night."

"Oh, Mama." She pulled away from me and stuffed more socks in the duffel. "It's not the dead of night. It's three o'clock, light as high noon."

"Well, it feels like dead of night! I'm completely worn out. I want you to stop packing—talk to me."

"There's nothing to talk about. I'll get a job, my own apartment....I'm grown up, Mama. You've done all you can do."

She went to the dresser. I walked over and blocked it.

"MOVE, MAMA!"

"Not until you listen to me. Sure, you'll get an apartment in a bad part of town. In a month you'll be thin and ragged, working at the Zippy Mart, wearing a blue smock with the name JILL emblazoned on the pocket, sit-ting behind a bullet-proof shield, embossing credit cards, skewering hot dogs on a rotisserie, pouring syrup into a Slurpee machine."

I could recite all this in my sleep. It was my own worst-possible-scenario.

I pressed on. "You'll be saving for months for class-es you can't afford, classes you have to put off from one month to the next, one year to the next, because the light bill's come due, or you're late with the rent. Oh, Jill, don't you see—all your old lightheartedness will be gone, all your dreams will be..."

"All right, Mama! Hush!"

"I'm just trying..."

"God! You've made your point. You sound like Mama Dean with her 'The-end-of-the-world-is-at-hand-and-there'll-be-weeping-and-wailing-and-gnashing-of-teeth-forever-and-ever, amen.'"

Once again, I was stung. Was that really how she saw me? "Well, Jill..."

"I'm sorry, Mama, but sometimes you make me crazy."

"I just want you to have a plan. Get a job—take summer classes with the Chief. By fall, you'll have some money saved, maybe a roommate to share expenses..."

"But fall's a million years off!"

I bit my lip. Fall *was* a million years off. I'd hoped to be leaving this weekend, myself. How could I ask Jill to stay when I wanted to leave?

I slumped on the bed. I didn't have the strength to fight her. If she really intended to leave, I couldn't stop her.

She stood there for a minute, then flopped down beside me. We both just stared at the wall, silent and miserable.

Finally she said, "What about Daddy?"

I sighed again. "Lord, Jill, I don't know. You'd be out of the house most of the time anyway."

I kept expecting her to get up and start packing again. But she just sat there sighing and staring.

Just when I thought we'd sit there staring and sighing on into eternity, she said, "Fall isn't *that* far off. It'd probably take me that long to move my stuff anyway."

I sat still, waiting to see where this was going.

"I've only saved a hundred dollars so far," she said.

I looked at her. "A hundred dollars! Where did you get a hundred dollars?"

"I sold some carvings at the flea market."

"A hundred dollars for carvings! You must be good."

She ducked her head, gave me a tired smile. "Yeah."

"You never once showed me your carvings," I said.

"You never asked."

"I'm asking now," I said.

"All right. But, you've got to promise to give up your Mama Dean routine," she said.

"Did I really sound like Mama Dean?"

She grinned, shoved the duffel bag off the bed. "Naw, I was just messing with you. I just said it 'cause I knew you were right and it burned me up. It got to you though, didn't it?"

I glanced at her, then looked away. "At first it got to me. But then I started to like it," I said.

She looked confused. "Mama?"

"Well, you've got to admit it, being a difficult woman will probably be my only inheritance," I said, straight-faced.

She looked at me another long minute.

"It's a joke, Jill. I was kidding."

"I know. But, you joking about Mama Dean. You didn't even look around to see if lightning was gonna strike you. You're changing, Mama—getting weird."

"Is that good?"

"I'm not sure. Yeah. I think so."

Already the air between us felt lighter. Everything was going to be all right. Downstairs a door banged. A second later, Steven's car started. I looked at the clock-radio.

"Daddy must be leaving to pick up Grandmother Presson."

Jill covered her face with a pillow. We both sighed, lost in our own thoughts.

Finally, she said, "All right, Mama. What's next?"

"First we go see your carvings. Then I'll start the Jello salads while you go to the school to clean up."

Jill's carvings filled the entire workshop. The minute she opened the door I came face to face with a huge cigar-store Indian. Next to him stood a totem pole, taller than me. Before I could get my bearings. Jill yanked me inside, flipped on a light, and locked the door behind us.

Three walls held makeshift shelves that went clear to the ceiling. They were jam-packed with carvings of small animals: squirrels, rabbits, foxes. A lower shelf held life-sized carving of heads—Indian children, chiefs, and squaws. Another shelf was loaded with every kind of bird from doves to fierce-eyed eagles. On the workbench was a basket filled to the brim with adobe houses the size of my fist.

I stood there staring, breathing in the scent of fresh-cut wood. I didn't jerk myself back to reality until Jill said, "Well, Mama?"

"I can't believe this! Fifty steps from the kitchen and I'm in a whole other world. How did you do all this?"

"I used the chain-saw, then an adz and a chisel on the big carvings. The little ones are mostly just whittled. What do you think, Mama? Do you like 'em?" Jill's voice was faint. She'd been holding her breath.

I put my hand on her shoulder. "Oh, Lord, Jill. Do I like them? I better than *like* them."

She grinned, then shrugged. "You have to say that. You're my mother. But they are starting to sell. 'Course, people like things that aren't that good...you know, owls with eye-glasses instead of real-looking owls; plastic country geese, with pink ribbons around their necks. Mrs. Overcash says to keep doing the adobe houses. They're my money-makers. They're so small I can whittle a couple after supper and carry a bunch of 'em in my duffel to the flea markets. I get five dollars apiece for them," she said, her eyes shining.

"Mrs. Overcash has seen your stuff?" I asked, trying to ignore a stab of jealousy.

"She's always at the flea markets. We talk."

"I wish you could have talked to me."

"Don't worry, Mama. I wasn't ready to show them to anyone in the family yet."

I looked around the room, touching everything. For awhile neither of us said anything. I picked up the carving of the old Indian woman's head and ran my fingers over her face. "I love this one. She has such deep, wise eyes, like she's seen every kind of heartache and heartbreak ever was."

"She's the shaman, Mama. The wise old medicine woman."

"Can I buy her?"

"Gosh, Mama. Are you sure you really want her?"

"Oh, yes!"

"I couldn't sell her to you. I'm not even sure if she's any good. But, if you really want her, you can have her."

I looked into my daughter's eyes, then into the face of the medicine woman.

"Oh, Jill. I think she's perfect just the way she is."

When we got back to the house, I set the shaman on the kitchen table. Then I noticed how late it was. Steven would be back with his mother and I hadn't even started the Jello salads. I laid out the ingredients: fruit, three kinds of Jello, mini-marshmallows, and coconut. Then I filled the tea kettle to boil water to dissolve the gelatin.

It wasn't 'til I set the kettle on the stove that I noticed the skillet of half-cooked potatoes I'd started for supper. The potatoes were gray and limp now, covered with grease that had gone cold hours before. On the counter, the package of fish sticks had thawed into a limp, oozing mass.

Our Steven-approved-every-other-Friday-night-menu.

Grabbing a trash bag, I scraped the potatoes and grease into it, then tossed in the package of fish sticks. On the way out the door, I stopped in front of the refrigerator, snatched the menu from its side, tore it into pieces, and carried the whole sorry mess outside to the garbage can.

Back inside, I started the Jello salads—celestial golden salad, pistachio-lime and sweet ambrosia.

It was late by the time the salads were cooling, so the girls and I ate fried bologna sandwiches at the kitchen table. Later, on my way up to bed, I carried the shaman into the front room, cleared Steven's magazines off the coffee table, and set the medicine-woman in the center.

Chapter Twenty-One

Graduation morning, I woke to a room as hot and airless as the inside of a closet. I could hear the low murmur of Steven's and Mother Presson's voices and the sounds of cupboard doors banging downstairs.

I lay there thinking about the day ahead. There was food to get ready, dishes to wash, last minute dusting and vacuuming, tables to set, relatives to greet. I wondered if Jerry would get his final decree today. Would he find a way to call me? Had Brenda managed to get the postponement she wanted? Did she still have the power to wear Jerry down—make him feel guilty, make him feel that he was supposed to stay with her? Twenty years ago she'd been fast and smart. Was Jerry really immune to fast, smart women—especially when the woman was his wife, the mother of his son? Oh, Lord.

It wasn't 'til I heard the girls' voices in the hallway that I slipped into my robe, brushed my hair, and pasted a smile on my face. If I started thinking about Jerry, I'd fall apart. The girls' graduation had to be the first order of the day.

Downstairs, Steven and Mother Presson were sitting at the dining room table, their heads together, whispering over croissants and Earl Grey tea. When they saw me, they jerked apart and looked so guilty that I went through to the kitchen without a word and tried not to notice that in spite of all that had happened, Steven still remembered croissants for his mother.

In the kitchen, Amy was standing over the ironing board pressing her graduation gown for the hundredth time. I was measuring coffee into a filter, when she threw the gown in a heap and flounced out of the room wailing, "No matter what I do it still looks like a rag!"

While the coffee was brewing, I looked out the kitchen window. Jill was sitting in the glider, under the magnolia, looking lost and alone. As soon as the coffee was ready, I took two mugs out to the glider, handed her one and said, "Today's the big day."

"I know," she said, ducking her head and grinning. "I can hardly believe it myself."

We sat there awhile, swinging and drinking coffee, until Amy came out on the back porch and yelled, "What are you doing, Mama? You've got to help me with this disgusting gown!"

So I went back inside and ironed the already smooth-as-glass-gown. Graduation day had started.

At two o'clock, I put on my navy dotted-Swiss shirtwaist and Mother and Mama Dean, Daddy and Willa Mae, Mother Presson, Steven and I, sat in the old auditorium watching the girls graduate.

Amy was solemn in her perfect white gown and pearls when Mr. Fentress announced that she'd won a scholarship to the University of North Carolina at Chapel Hill. I wondered if she'd really leave tacky us and tacky Poplar Grove behind forever.

Then, Jill (in her wrinkled gown) stepped onto the stage and flashed a grin and a peace sign. When she accepted her diploma, I wondered if the ink on it had had time to dry.

I had promised myself I wouldn't cry, but I almost choked when they crossed the stage. Mother, Mama Dean, and Mother Presson were dabbing their eyes quietly, and Daddy reached over to squeeze my hand. Everyone around me was holding hands and sniffing. But when I looked at Steven, he was staring straight ahead. That's when my eyes welled up. We should have been sharing this moment together.

Later, when the ceremony was over, we rode in silence back to the house for the party.

Mother and Willa Mae helped me in the kitchen while Mama Dean nagged Daddy into carrying the Wallbanger cake, jars of sun tea, and gifts from her car. Then she forced him to move all the dining room furniture, the big table, six heavy chairs, the folding table and four folding chairs—everything but the buffet and hutch—to the opposite end of the room. When that arrangement didn't suit her, she fussed at him 'til he moved everything back to where it had been in the first place.

While all this was going on, Steven and Mother Presson took their ease on the front porch, drinking iced tea and acting like Lord and Lady of the Plantation.

A few minutes later Mary Price and Hoyt pulled into the driveway in their Silverado, followed by Theo Bloodworth's gray Lincoln Town Car.

After everyone arrived, congratulated the girls and laid their gifts on the table, I carried a tray of ice tea and punch to the front room.

Theo and Mother Presson were sitting side by side on the couch. I saw Mother Presson pick up Jill's carving and turn it over to check the label.

I carried the tray to them and said, "Jill made that."

They both ignored me, so I set down the tray and

said louder, "Jill made that."

Mother Presson looked at me. "Did you say something, Margaret?"

"The carving, Mother Presson. Jill made it. See the initials JP on the bottom," I said, turning it over.

Mother Presson stared at me. "Surely you don't mean *our* Jill?"

"She's been working in the garage workshop all year. She's made hundreds of carvings."

"Well, Maggie, no one ever mentioned..." Mother Presson said coolly.

Theo said, "Excuse me, Maggie. Did you say this is *your* Jill's carving?"

By now, Theo and Mother Presson were pulling their reading glasses from their purses to get a better look.

"It's an Indian shaman. A wise old medicinewoman," I said, like I'd known it all along.

"Why, I had no idea that Jill could...but it's charming, " Mother Presson stammered.

"It positively speaks to me," Theo said. "It's so powerful—primitive, almost...primordial."

"Jill's just a beginner," I said.

"But, Maggie. It being primitive is what makes it so stunning. I can't believe I've been coming here for years and no one ever told me we had a budding artist in our midst," Theo said.

"Well, I intend to find out about this. Where's Steven?" Mother Presson's nostrils were flaring.

Just then Steven strolled into the room, wearing his pink, gracious-host look.

Theo linked arms with him and walked him to the coffee table. "Modesty's one thing, Steven, but how long did you plan to keep this a secret?"

Steven looked pleased, then confused.

"Really, Steven," Mother Presson said. "I feel a perfect fool. Is a man completely without honor in his own country?"

Steven smiled nervously. "What are you talking about?"

"For goodness sake, Steven. I'm talking about Jill—the carving. *Jill's* carving. My grand-daughter is gifted and no one ever told me. Why, she's wasting herself here in Poplar Grove. She must come to Chapel Hill with me immediately where her gifts will get the attention they deserve."

Steven looked blank.

Mother Presson sighed loudly and handed him the shaman.

Steven looked at the carving, then at Mother Presson and Theo. It was clear he still didn't know what they were talking about.

Theo smiled. "I'm so impressed, Steven. What art school is Jill attending?"

Steven blinked. "Art school?"

Mother Presson sniffed and fanned herself with a napkin. "Why only this morning Steven-The-Educator planned to send our little Rodin to computer school."

"Now, Mother. I didn't know...I mean, I knew Jill was out in the workshop doing *something*. But she's always up to something. I figured it was one of her whims. She's always had these odd whims."

"She's not quite eighteen. If she can't have a few whims now when can she have whims?" I snapped.

Steven blinked again. "Of course she can have whims, if we all recognize that they *are* whims. She might have a certain raw talent, but, she never follows through with anything. At least computer school is something concrete—something *real*. I want her to have something to fall back on when she gets bored with this current... uh...whim."

"Chief Too-Tall has agreed to take her on as a student," I said.

Everyone looked at me.

"Really, Margaret," Mother Presson said. "She must go to an accredited art school. I can't believe you'd consider some local lout...and Steven's idea of computer school...well, Jill is truly wasting herself with the pair of you."

My face and neck went hot. But before I could defend myself, Theo patted her perfect chignon and said smoothly, "Mrs. Presson, Chief Too-Tall *is* local so you're probably not familiar with his work. But I assure you he's a master carver. I have a few of his works myself. It's really quite an honor that he'd take Jill on at her young age...though seeing her work, I can understand why he'd make an exception."

Theo smiled up at Steven. "I know what you're doing, Steven. It's hard for doting daddies to let go of their little girls. Why, when I wanted to back-pack across Europe after my graduation my poor daddy was horrified! He wanted me safe, here by his side in Poplar Grove. The artist's life is difficult and Jill *is* young, but you mustn't be too overprotective. You have to let her try her wings."

Instead of feeling chastised or embarrassed, doting-daddy Steven blushed to his roots and smiled at Theo in a way he'd never smiled at me. Steven and Theo? Theo and Steven? But before I could think of the word "wavelength," Theo floated out of the room in a cloud of good perfume and rustling silk.

Mother Presson said, "My, what a charming woman. It's a relief to know there are such people here in Poplar Grove—that Jill won't be casting her pearls entirely before swine."

After we ate, Theo and Mother Presson talked Jill into letting everyone tour her workshop. When they were through, everyone in the family swore that Jill got her talent from their side.

Later, when Steven and Mother Presson announced that not only would Jill be going to art school, she'd also be taking summer classes from the Chief, Jill rushed into the kitchen, shouting, "God, Mama, did you hear the news? I can't believe it! I swear I cannot believe it!"

Then, before I could hug her, she slipped out the back door and spent the rest of the day following Steven, Theo, and Mother Presson around like a puppy and hanging onto their every word.

Washing party dishes, I stood at the kitchen window and watched them, feeling completely left out.

Just when I was considering pinching the head off the one surviving African violet, Mary Price carried a plate into the kitchen.

"Lord, Maggie Sweet," she said. "Who would have thought it! Jill actually graduated! And now with her art work, everyone thinks the sun shines out of her pinkie-finger. Why, she's gone from being a juvenile delinquent to an artist in one day."

I didn't answer, just banged the dishes into the sink and ran the hot water full force.

Mary Price turned off the faucet and looked at me. "Well, Lord, Maggie! Don't break a sweat or anything. I thought you'd be thrilled."

"I *am* thrilled. It's just...I've been on her side all

along. But the minute Steven shows any interest—does what he should have been doing all along—I'm supposed to stand up and cheer, break out in a rash or something. Jill's following him around like he's the second coming," I said, feeling hot tears behind my eyes.

"Oh, Lord!" Mary Price leaned against the counter, lit a Virginia Slim, and tossed the burnt-out match in the direction of the sink.

"I know it's hard, Maggie. But, you'll just have to get over it. You're right. Jill *has* had you on her side. She's never had to give that a second thought. But the thing is, what she's always craved is having her daddy on her side. *His* attention. You've been a good mother. The best. But your girls are moving on with their lives. You've mostly done all you can for them."

I stared out the window. Maybe Mary Price was right. Maybe I *had* done all I could do for my girls. It had just never come to me that Jill would trade me for art school.

Chapter Twenty-Two

Saturday morning, Steven, Mother Presson and the girls left for Chapel Hill. For their graduation gift, Mother Presson planned to take the girls clothing shopping, then to an art museum and on to dinner at a fancy restaurant. I pleaded a headache and after-party clean-up and stayed home, hoping to hear from Jerry.

On the way out the door, Steven mumbled something about spending the night at Mother Presson's if it got too late.

After they left, I settled in at the kitchen table with a third cup of coffee, a cigarette and the newspaper. Just when I was thinking about getting dressed, an article on the front page caught my eye:

POPLAR GROVE WOMAN SAYS HAIR
"MELTED" AFTER PROCESS

Blondelle Ashburn says she wanted her hair curled, not fried. So she's suing the Beauty Box after most of her hair fell out.

Ms. Ashburn, 45, is suing the Beauty Box for $10,000, the maximum the law allows.

According to Ms. Ashburn's suit, Jewel Hollifield from the Beauty Box gave her a permanent, but also attended other customers during the process.

"They left it on too long! When I got home I felt sharp

pains in my scalp, but when I tried to rinse it out, my hair just melted and ran right down the drain. I was completely bald on the right side. Then, at supper that night, the whole left side fell out, right into my pinto beans. I like to have died when that happened."

The Beauty Box, located at the Port City Mall, Poplar Grove, will be closed until further notice.

I'd barely finished reading the article when the telephone rang.

"You've got to get down here! It's a matter of life and death!" Shirley shouted. Then, before I could ask the first question, she hung up.

I ran upstairs, threw on my clothes, looked at the phone one last time, and drove uptown faster than the law allows.

When I pulled up in front of The Curl & Swirl, the parking lot was full.

There were women sitting in their cars, others waiting on the porch and more sitting on the stair-steps.

When I finally got inside, Shirley, who was usually calm and slow moving, looked like a televangelist on a mission from God.

"Did you read the paper?" She asked.

"I was reading it when you called. I can't believe it!"

"I know. I've been wishing this for years. But, like Mama always said, 'be careful what you wish for, your wish might come true.'"

"Well, Shirley, you ought to be thrilled!"

"I am thrilled. It's just that everyone from here to Silver City picked today to have a hair crisis. I need you to work all day, if you can! Lurleen's in the bathroom having a nervous breakdown and that Dixie left for a breakfast order at Hardee's and never came back. I swear, Mama's nearly eighty and she's more help in crisis than those two."

Just then, Mrs. Mabes came out of the back room, grinned and waved a teasing comb at me.

"Mama's in her glory," Shirley said. "She's already shampooed and Dippity-Dood anything that don't move. I know she's thinking maybe we can be number one again. But Lord at the timing. I was already booked solid with the Spivey wedding and without telling me, Mama set up appointments for all the Freewill Baptist ladies for their bus tour of Charlotte tomorrow."

Shirley wasn't exaggerating. There were women under dryers, women sitting and dripping waiting for a dryer—not to mention all those still waiting outside. For a second I thought about what Steven would say. Then I remembered that Steven was in Chapel Hill!

"Lead me to a smock and chair. I'll stay as long as you need me," I said.

A few minutes later, Lurleen came out of the bathroom and Dixie returned from Hardee's claiming a flat tire. Shirley mapped out a plan and we all set to work. Shirley, Dixie and Lurleen doing sets and comb-outs, Mrs. Mabes making coffee and fussing over the customers and me cutting hair.

Even though we were too busy to take more than one breath at a time, I grinned the whole day.

At noon, we quit taking walk-ins. But, even so, it was seven o'clock before I powdered the neck of my last customer.

We were all cleaning up our sections and talking about the day when Modine, Doris, and Jessie Rae Moore came into the shop.

"We're fixing to close, ladies," Shirley said, sweeping hair into a pile.

"Oh, we're not here to get our hair done." Modine said.

"It's just...we've heard some news that can't wait," Doris said.

We came right down—wanted you to be the first to know," Modine said.

We all stopped what we were doing and looked at them.

Doris took a deep breath. "I went down to Nims' Hardware this morning and the store was closed..."

"That should have told us something...Nims' never closes...It's Bucky's motto—Nims' Never Closes," Modine interrupted.

"Well, it did seem kind of odd, but I shoved it to the back of my mind, you know, like you do when you're busy. Then, tonight I was calling around town to find out where I need to drop Mama off for her bus tour of Charlotte in the morning..."

"Lord, Doris, cut to the chase. My feet are killing me," Shirley said.

"Well, that's when I heard it," Doris said. "Bucky Nims has gone and left Dreama!"

"What?" Shirley shouted.

"Not Bucky Nims. Why he'd never..." Dixie, Lurleen and I said in unison.

"Bullshit and applesauce," Mrs. Mabes said.

"It's true," Modine said.

Shirley sat down hard in her chair. "Now, you all, repeat that and say it real slow, but don't tell me something like that if it ain't true. My nerves just can't take it."

"It's true all right," Doris said. "Like I said, I was

calling around for Mama and got it straight from Harvel Pollard at the Trailways Bus Depot. Harvel said Bucky just packed his things and left a note saying, 'I told you I was leaving. Now I'm gone.' Then he took the first bus out of town."

"It happened yesterday—right after that pasty-faced girl of theirs graduated," Modine added.

"He musta had it planned for years. To leave out so quick," Shirley said.

"Lord, Lord. I didn't know he had it in him," Dixie said, her voice filled with wonder.

"Still waters run deep," Lurleen said.

"It's the quiet ones that bear watching," Jessie Rae said, biting her lip.

"Well, I hope he went further than a Trailways bus could take him. His life won't be worth a plug nickel when Dreama and that girl of hers catch up with him," Mrs. Mabes said.

"Maybe they won't catch him, Mama," Shirley said.

"Oh, they'll catch him all right. They won't rest 'til they catch him," Mrs. Mabes nodded wisely.

"Lord, Mama, can't we enjoy this for one minute?" Shirley asked.

"All I'm saying is, I know what I know. They'll catch him all right and when they do his life won't be worth spit," Mrs. Mabes went on.

Shirley rolled her eyes. "Go on, Doris. Mama's just being a killjoy."

"They say Dreama's taking it right hard—she's took to her bed. Why the shock alone like to have killed her. I drove by her house and all the shades were drawn," Doris said.

"Ashamed to show her face," Modine said.

"Bullshit and applesauce. That woman don't have no shame," Mrs. Mabes said.

"What Bucky did was the bravest thing I ever heard of and I surely hope he gets away," Jessie Rae said. Then her eyes darted everywhere. "Oh, my, that sounded so ugly...I only meant...."

"It's all right, Jessie Rae. We know what you meant," everyone said.

"Anyway, we figured after Shirley chasing Dreama out of her shop and Dreama fixing to ruin all y'alls' lives...well, we figured you all deserved to be the first to know," Doris said.

"Shirley, I want you to know, I think you chasing Dreama off and all, well, I think that's the bravest thing I ever heard of," Jessie Rae said. "And Maggie Sweet, I think you wearing that precision-cut and working at The Curl & Swirl, when everyone knows how Steven feels about it...well, I think it's the bravest thing I ever..."

"Thanks Jessie Rae," I said.

Everyone stared at Jessie Rae. It was the most we'd ever heard her say.

Her eyes darted everywhere, but she went on. "Sometimes, I get so timid and tongue-tied I wonder why you all even bother with me. But, Maggie Sweet, I've been thinking about some things. I'm nearly forty years old and I've never done anything the least bit brave...so I figured I'd start with one of those precision cuts and a little of that #104 hair-color. And I'd like you to set me up an appointment...you know, if it isn't too much trouble."

I looked at Shirley. I wasn't sure if I was an official Curl & Swirl employee.

Shirley winked and handed me the appointment book.

A second later, she disappeared into the back room and returned with a dusty, green bottle.

"It's old, it's cheap and it's room temperature. But it *is* champagne," she said.

When she opened the bottle, the cork hit the ceiling so hard it stuck. Everyone shrieked.

After she'd divided the champagne into eight Styrofoam cups, she raised her cup and said, "We need to celebrate! Bucky Nims lives. The Curl & Swirl lives. And Maggie Sweet and Jessie Rae are fixing to start a new life. I swanee, some days the universe is just slap full of surprises!"

It was late when I left The Curl and Swirl. All in the world I wanted to do was get home, take a long soak in a hot tub and crawl into bed.

But when I pulled into the driveway, Steven's car was there.

For a second, I panicked—unbuttoned my smock to hide it under the car seat. Then I thought about Jessie Rae calling me brave. No one had called me brave in years. I thought back to the little girl who'd wanted her nickname to be Scout. What had happened to her? What had happened to Daddy's 'Rebel', his 'feisty little brown haired girl'?

I took a deep breath and got out of the car.

When I opened the door, Steven called from the kitchen, "I was just about to call the State Highway Patrol! The girls decided to stay with Mother, but I had work to do." He rounded the corner into the front room, spotted my smock and stood stock still. "Dammit, Maggie! You've been working at The Curl & Swirl, haven't you?"

"Yes. I...."

"The breakfast dishes are still on the table You must have gone down there the minute we left this morning. No wonder you wouldn't go with us. You'd planned this all along. Well, I won't have it. I've told you over and over again that no wife of mine is ever going to work!"

I didn't think. I just blurted out, "I can't do this anymore, Steven. I won't. You're not my daddy. I don't need your *permission*."

Then I walked out the door and drove to the center of town and checked myself in to the Yadkin Motel, on Main Street, next door to the Zippy Mart—fifteen dollars a night, no questions asked.

I felt reckless and happy, strong enough to handle anything.

I was barely settled in my room when the telephone rang. "Maggie Sweet, have you lost your only mind?"

"Steven! How in the world did you find me?"

"You're staying in a motel on Main Street, next door to the Zippy Mart. Everyone in town knows where you are! I've already had two calls. I'll give you five minutes to get home."

"I won't be home. I've gone and left you, Steven."

He gasped at the other end. For a few seconds the phone seemed to go dead. I was just about to hang up when he sputtered, "You can't do that. You've got children. You've got responsibilities."

"I'll take care of my responsibilities. But I'm not coming home."

"I'm warning you, Maggie! Five minutes!"

I didn't bother to argue. Hanging up was the easiest thing in the world to do.

Ten minutes later he was pounding on my door.

I opened the door as far as the chain-lock allowed. "What do you want?"

"I want to know what's come over you. I want to know why you're determined to humiliate me?"

"I'm not out to humiliate you."

"Dammit, Maggie..."

"We haven't been happy for years. I want a divorce."

He brushed his hand across his forehead like he was completely worn out. "I never thought you'd do this to us."

My eyes welled. I fumbled with the chain-lock, opened the door. "I never thought I would either, Steven. It's just...no one should have to live with someone who doesn't love them—someone they don't love."

"You're being ridiculous. What's worse is you're making *me* look ridiculous. If you don't care about me and the children, what about your mother and Mama Dean? Any minute now their phone will start ringing too. I never thought you'd do this to them."

I took a deep breath. I'd rather take a beating than have Mother or Mama Dean come to the Yadkin. Then it hit me: Steven was threatening me with mother and Mama Dean to keep me in line. To make me do what he wanted. "If it'll make you feel better, I'll call Mother and Mama Dean myself," I bluffed.

He looked at me like my hair was on fire. Then he grabbed my arm, and started hauling me across the parking lot toward his car.

Now, I'm not the type to make a scene in public and Steven knows it. But the minute I got one arm free, I snatched his good Cross pen and pencil set from his shirt pocket, and stomped on them. It was the only thing I could think to do.

Steven just stood there with his mouth gaping open, staring at his pen and pencil set sticking out of the blacktop.

Then the traffic light in front of the motel turned

red and several cars stopped. Everyone was craning their necks watching us scuffle.

"Steven! Those people in the cars are watching us. They think you're trying to kidnap me or something," I hissed.

Well, Steven was so mortified, he let go my arm and smiled a sickly smile in the direction of the cars to show he was harmless. Then he picked up the pieces of his pen and pencil set, got in his car, and drove off.

I ran back to my room completely worn out.

For awhile, I sat on the patched chenile bedspread, aggravated enough to scream. A person couldn't even leave her own husband without everyone in this town getting in on it.

Staying at the Yadkin was not going to work. I'd only left home for a half hour, and Steven had already been down here, all because certain people couldn't mind their own business.

In an hour, half the town would be parading through the parking lot, knocking on my door, offering advice, taking sides between Steven and me.

I thought about Mother and Mama Dean. Steven was right. They'd be down here any minute. And Dreama Nims! Why, she'd get off her deathbed to witness my dis-grace.

I picked up my purse, left a message on Mary Price's message machine, and drove to the only place in this world I could go.

Chapter Twenty-Three

I hadn't been on I-40 fifteen minutes when I knew I'd made the biggest mistake of my life. It had all happened so fast. One minute I'd been standing on the side of a hill and the next minute I was rolling down the hill, going too fast to know where or when I'd stop. I'd left my family! What if Jerry never came back? What if I'd left my family only to live on the streets like a bag lady? I wasn't sure if I had a job; I didn't have a place to live. I'd disgraced everyone—ruined my life.

Now I was speeding down the Interstate to Daddy's and didn't even know what I'd say when I got there. When I passed the Chapel Hill city limits sign, I decided to tell Daddy and Willa Mae that I'd just stopped by for a visit. Later, I'd break it to them that I'd left Steven.

But by the time I got to Daddy's, I was in such a state that I threw myself into his arms and wailed, "Oh, Daddy, I've gone and left home."

And Daddy said, "Now, sugar. It'll be all right. Everything's gonna be all right," just as calm as if me showing up in the middle of the night, dressed in a pink Curl & Swirl smock was the most normal thing in the world!

Later, when I settled down, Willa Mae loaned me a nightgown and I crawled into bed in my old room.

I was almost asleep when I overheard Daddy talking on the phone.

"Well, Steven, I just thought I'd let you know she's safe. Now, there's no sense carrying on so. You knew how it was when you married her. It's in her blood. Why, her Mama Dean Pruitt run her grand-daddy off and her mama run me off, too. I guess it's a pure wonder Maggie stuck around as long as she did, bless her heart. The thing is, Steven, she just couldn't help herself."

I sat up straight in the bed. No wonder Daddy wasn't surprised to see me. He'd been expecting me for nineteen years!

I sat there in the dark, listening to Daddy explain women to Steven—especially Pruitt women. Women were treacherous. That's just how they were. It went along with the xx female chromosomes and couldn't be helped any more than flat feet or color blindness. 'Course me having Pruitt blood in my veins made me doubly treacherous. Why, according to Daddy, Steven ought to thank his lucky stars that I wasn't all Pruitt. If I'd been *pure* raging Pruitt and not watered-down with Daddy's forgiving, reasonable Sweet blood, Steven wouldn't be sleeping safely in his bed tonight. A pure Pruitt woman would have run *him* off.

Before he hung up, Daddy said, "'Course I won't be listening to nothing bad about my girl, nor have you bothering her, either one. If she said divorce, well, that's it. It's been good talking to you too, Steven. Uh huh. Good-bye."

It was the oddest thing, lying in bed in the guest room, hearing Daddy explain me that way. I probably should have felt insulted But that was exactly why I'd come here. Steven would never follow me here. Daddy's odd, stubborn logic had always confused and infuriated him.

But mostly I'd come here because no matter what happened, I knew that Daddy loved me warts and all.

Sunday morning, after breakfast, I walked down to the creek behind Daddy's property. The sky was a cloudless blue, the color of pre-washed jeans. I sat on a rock and stared into the creek, thinking back to that long-ago summer when I came here to smoke on the sly and brood about Jerry.

Nothing had changed. Here I was, twenty years later, doing the same thing—smoking on the sly and brooding about Jerry. Was I in some kind of time warp? Or was it one of those universal things Shirley talked about—coming full circle?

I reached in my pocket and pulled out a cigarette and a piece of paper fluttered to the ground.

Jerry's poem. I took a deep breath, unfolded the paper and read it, my eyes lingering over the words, "he finds his soul where he left it/ with the girl at Belews Pond. I loved you then. I love you now. I will always love you."

I sat there awhile and let the tears fall. Then I wiped them with the backs of my hands, took a deep breath and headed back toward the house.

As I walked over the rise, I saw Jerry's pick-up in the driveway.

He was at the table drinking Daddy's thick, strong coffee. I'd never been so glad to see anyone in my life. Then he was whirling me around, lifting me off my feet and shouting, "We did it! We did it! I can't believe we did it!"

"Lord, Jerry! I can't believe you're here!" I said, holding on tight.

"I got home last night and didn't know how to reach you. So I went down to the Palomino. Mary Price said she'd call you and call me back. She didn't call till 3 a.m.—the minute she got home. She'd heard your phone message that you'd left Steven. Lord, honey, it was all I could do not to drive here then and there. I just didn't know how your dad would take it."

"He come here half an hour ago to ask for your hand. I was just asking him about his prospects," Daddy said.

"His prospects? Lord, Daddy!" I said.

"Now, Maggie, this is between us men-folk," Daddy said.

"It is not! It's between Jerry and me."

"Well, now, there you go, Jerry. I told you she was feisty."

"I can see that, sir." Jerry grinned at me.

"It's plain to see how you all feel about one another. But it's a daddy's job to talk about prospects," Daddy said, giving Jerry a friendly man-to-man nudge.

In nineteen years I'd never seen him nudge Steven.

"Well, Mr. Sweet, it's like this..." Jerry started.

"Call me Jack. Smiling Jack. Every time you say Mr. Sweet I look around expectin' to see *my* daddy," Daddy said.

"All right, Jack. To tell you the truth, I just got my clock cleaned pretty good in my divorce..."

"So, money was the name of her game," I said.

Willa Mae poured fresh coffee and set huge slabs of peach pie in front of everyone.

"Money was always the name of her game. But I've still got the farmhouse and the truck...that and my Navy pension. Uh, thanks, Mrs. Sweet," Jerry said.

"Maggie'll have to work then?" Daddy asked.

"I want to work. I've already got a job," I said.

"You did? When?" Jerry asked.

"Yesterday. I started working at The Curl & Swirl."

"It's all falling into place," Jerry said, squeezing my hand.

"Well, it takes two a'working just to make it these days. Why, Willa Mae and me worked at that old hosiery mill for years and...you say you own a farmhouse?" Daddy said, looking up from his pie.

"Yes, sir...uh, Jack. It's an old farmhouse—only a couple of acres of land. But it's got the prettiest pond behind it... and lots of out buildings. I plan to start a carpentry business," Jerry said.

"He's good, too, Daddy. Wait'll you see the farmhouse. He's built cupboards, counter tops, a new porch..."

"Is the pond stocked?" Daddy asked, ignoring me.

"There's bream and bass and catfish...I don't know what all. You're welcome to try your luck any time," Jerry said.

We all dug into our pie. Daddy and Willa Mae, Jerry and me. It all seemed so natural, I could already picture Daddy loading his pick up with fishing poles and flies, spending weekends with us at the farmhouse.

Outside, Jerry put his arms around me. "God, I missed you!"

"It seemed like forever."

"It *was* forever. Want me to follow you home?"

"I'll follow you. I've got a lot of thinking to do."

"I love you to pieces."

"I think you hung the moon."

Chapter Twenty-Four

Over the next two weeks, I realized that I'd been a fool to think it was all over but the shouting. There hadn't been any shouting, but it was still far from over.

I was in such high gear the afternoon I left Daddy's that I drove directly to Mother and Mama Dean's. But when I tried to talk to them, Mama Dean went to bed with a sick headache. Then Mother's face seemed to crumble and she said, "I can't talk about this now, Maggie," and she rushed to *her* room. After two weeks they still wouldn't talk about it. To tell you the truth, they were barely speaking to me at all.

I hadn't talked to my girls yet either. I phoned and drove by the house dozens of times but no one was ever at home. Then I heard through Shirley who'd heard through Theo Bloodworth that Steven had picked them up at his mother's and taken them to Myrtle Beach. This flew all over me! For years I'd begged him to take us to Myrtle Beach, but he just glared at me, wouldn't even discuss it. It was bad enough I wasn't able to see my girls, but worse that he had time (and the beach) to convince them he was Father-of-the-Year and I was "Mommy Dearest."

Just thinking about my family made my eyes well and my stomach clench.

As if I wasn't already stressed out, the night came for the Poplar Grove class of 1965's 20th class reunion at the Moose Club.

So much had happened in just two weeks. I'd gone and left Steven and everyone knew it. I was working at the The Curl & Swirl and living in the apartment behind the shop. Jerry and I were together, just not officially together.

But everyone had to be thinking, "Isn't it odd that after all those years, Maggie left Steven the minute Jerry Roberts hit town?"

If we went to the reunion everyone would be watching. One false move and our secret would be out and they'd all think we were heathens.

On the other hand, it would look even more suspicious if we both cancelled. Besides, we'd have to show our faces in public sooner or later.

At the farmhouse, the night before the reunion, it all seemed so complicated, I broke down and cried. Jerry held me in his arms and said, "It's all right, Maggie. It's going to be all right. We just have to take it one day at a time."

So, we *did* decide to go the reunion. We'd just go separately, blend in with the crowd, then sit at the same table. You know, sort of let us sneak up gradually, a little at a time, until folks accepted us as a couple.

I only hoped I could pull it off.

As I drove to the Moose Club, I told myself, over and over again, "Take a deep breath. Don't panic. You can do this if you don't panic."

I'd just parked my car when I saw Mary Price and Hoyt's Silverado circling the parking lot. Mary Price waved and got out of the truck and while Hoyt drove off to find an empty spot, she walked me inside.

She waited with me in the lobby until I was pretty sure I could walk and breathe at the same time. Then she took my arm and said, "I promise you, Maggie, you really will live right through this."

The next thing I knew we were sitting at a long table with our old high school crowd: Modine and Ellis, Geneva and Knoxie, Toy and Bobby. Hoyt had met Jerry in the parking lot. Since they were the last to arrive, the only seats left were at the opposite end of the table.

Everyone's eyes darted from Jerry to me, from me to Jerry as they tried to make small talk. The men talked about the gas mileage of pick-ups versus mini-vans. The women talked about their children, their new reunion outfits, and the people at the other tables. Now and then there'd be a long awkward pause and everyone rushed in to fill the silence with comments about the weather or to mention, once again, that the hall was decorated in red and gray crepe paper streamers, Poplar Grove's school colors.

I tried to act normal but my face felt hot and stiff.

When the DJ started playing golden oldies: "Let's Twist Again, Like We Did Last Summer," "Love, Love Me, Do," "Wake Up, Little Suzie," "Bad, Bad, Leroy Brown," everyone relaxed. Soon we were singing along with the music and laughing about the things we got up to in high school.

Now and then, Jerry's blue eyes met mine across the crowded table and I'd think, he fits in. It's like he never left.

I danced with Ellis, then Knoxie and Bobby, while Jerry danced with their wives. Then everyone crowded the floor for the "Hokey Pokey" and the "Bunny Hop."

After we ate (we had barbecued ribs and chicken and twice baked potatoes, catered by Millie's Percolator Grill), the DJ played "In The Still Of The Night." I was dancing with Hoyt when he came up behind me.

"Hey, old buddy, mind if I cut in?"

Hoyt made a deep courtly bow, and all at once I was in Jerry's arms.

I laid my head on his chest, then jerked away. "Oh, Lord, I forgot."

"I know." He stepped back, looked into my eyes. "But we've danced with everyone else. If we don't dance together, it'll look like we're avoiding each other. Now smile and say, sha doop, sha doop, de doop."

"Why?"

"Because it's the only line I know. Because you're in my arms and I don't want to forget we're in public."

I smiled. "Sha doop da doop de doop. I wish we were at the farmhouse."

"We will be and soon."

"You think so?"

"I know so."

Toy and Bobby Overcash danced past us, then Modine and Ellis. Jerry smiled. "Sha doop, de doop." For a moment they just stared at us, then Bobby smiled and Ellis nodded.

"You think they know?'"

He shrugged. "Probably."

"Oh, Lord."

"They're our friends, Maggie. We go back a long way."

I stared out into the crowd. We *did* go back a long way. Hoyt and Mary Price, Modine and Elllis, Bobby and Toy. Everyone in this room really. We'd been children together, grown up together. We'd been in and out of each other's houses, knew each other's parents, grandparents, and children. Memories washed over me, memories of grade school and ceiling fans, playing tag and Red-Rover at recess. Then high school and Dixie Burger, Tangee and dating. I remembered cook-outs and christenings; the months we stuck close to Doris when Knoxie was missing in Viet Nam; the time we carried cash and casseroles when it looked like Modine and Ellis would lose their farm. We'd celebrated and cried together and even when we didn't agree we'd been there for each other.

But before I could tell Jerry what I was thinking, the music changed from "In The Still Of The Night" to "Goodnight Ladies."

Everyone moved to the floor for the last dance. A few minutes later we returned to our tables to pick up purses and sweaters and souvenir matches.

It wasn't until we were all standing in the parking lot saying our goodbyes that it hit me—the reunion was over and I *had* lived right through it.

Later, as I followed Jerry back to the farmhouse, I thought about what lay ahead. Steven's anger. Explaining us to the girls. The year-long wait for a divorce to become final in North Carolina. I thought about Mother and Mama Dean. The two I dreaded facing the most. It would probably take a lifetme to make it up to them.

Up ahead, Jerry motioned toward a DETOUR sign. For the next two or three miles, the road was so rutted and filled with pot holes, I wondered if my old car would make it.

Then suddenly the road smoothed out and we passed the Dingler's farmhouse, the stand of loblolly pines, then Belews Pond. That's when I remembered what Daddy said on the phone that night, two weeks ago.

When it came to to talking to Mother and Mama

Dean, I'd have to remind them it's in the blood—that leaving a husband seems to run in the family.

So I tucked my car behind Jerry's pick-up and settled in for the ride. Maggie and Jerry, together, 4-ever, right here in Poplar Grove and real life.